# I'll Settle for Love

## Michelle Lynn Brown

# I'll Settle for Love - Book Three in the Trampled Rose Series

Michelle Lynn Brown

Copyright © 2013 Michelle Lynn Brown


Cover Design by Michelle Lynn Brown
Image © stefanolunardi (Stefano Lunardi) / Bigstock Photo
Image © luckyraccoon (Dmytro Panchenko) / Bigstock Photo
Image © Anelina / Bigstock Photo
Image © Eky Studio / Bigstock Photo


Scripture quotations are taken from the Holy Bible, New Living Translation, copyright ©1996, 2004, 2007 by Tyndale House Foundation. Used by permission of Tyndale House Publishers, Inc., Carol Stream, Illinois 60188. All rights reserved.

No part of this publication may be reproduced in any form, stored in any retrieval system, posted on any website, or transmitted in any form without written permission from the publisher, except for brief quotations in printed reviews and articles.

This book is a work of fiction. Names, characters, places, and incidents are the product of the author's imagination and are used fictitiously. Any resemblance to locations, actual events, or persons, either living or dead, is coincidental.

*For my beautiful daughter, Michaella. You are an inspiration. Thank you for always reminding me to look deeper than someone's actions.*

*For my mother-in-law, Teena. Thank you for always reflecting Christ's love, grace and mercy.*

Acknowledgements:

This book would not have been possible without the wonderful editing talents of Nat Davis of Davis Professionals. Your patience, honesty and expertise have been a blessing to me!

Thank you to the members of the Christian Indie Authors group. The group's willingness to share their wisdom, advice and painful experiences made this book possible.

I would also like to thank the American Military Families Autism Support community. As a mother of an autistic daughter and a military spouse, this community has helped me get through my toughest days. Thank you for your support as I gathered research for this book.

I pray that every word of this book encourages, uplifts and guides the readers to a closer, intimate relationship with our Lord, Jesus Christ.

When I have learnt to love God better than my earthly dearest, I shall love my earthly dearest better than I do now.

C.S. Lewis

# Prologue

"This is my fault." The young woman whispered as she struggled to sit up on the hospital bed. Those were the first words she had spoken since they arrived. The strong smell of antiseptic burned her nostrils.

"Lee-Lee, there's no reason for tears." The man laid his hand on the small of the young woman's back. She stiffened at his touch.

His next words came out in an exasperated whisper. "At least the problem is taken care of."

She placed a trembling hand over her mouth and turned her head. She wanted to yell at him that this wasn't a problem, but her conscience cut her words short. Hadn't she been praying for all of it to disappear? Hadn't she referred to this situation as a nightmare? She was no better than *him*; she felt like vomiting.

He gently ran the back of his hand down her cheek, and a violent shudder racked her body. "No one needs to know about this little visit to the hospital." His tone held a sugar coated threat. "This is our secret."

The sound of the metal hooks on the privacy curtain scraping against the rod caused the man to quickly tuck his hand into his pocket.

The doctor breezed in, looking at her chart. He looked up and said to her, "You can go home now. Make sure you get lots bed rest, no lifting..."

The doctor's words became dull and fuzzy as the wave of nausea that had been threatening to surface finally erupted. She threw up all over the man's pants.

The doctor stuck his head out from the side of the curtain, calling for an orderly as the man stared down in astonished disgust at the vomit dripping down the side of his leg.

A part of her wanted to smile at the look of revulsion on his face. *Serves him right!* But dizziness washed over her and she looked down to see blood staining the front of her gown where it rested between her legs. She felt as if she were floating away from her body, barely aware of herself falling back on the hospital bed.

## Six Years Later

"Lee-Lee, you make a beautiful bride."

Leanne hated that nickname. She didn't look at her stepfather as she stiffly said "thank you." Though the two appeared to glide effortlessly across the ballroom, the dance was stiff, quiet, and awkward for both parties.

"My baby is all grown up." The man's voice was a soft murmur.

Their eyes locked for a moment, and Leanne withdrew a dollop of courage hidden deep within her. "I am not *your* baby." Her words were just as soft as his, but they came out with an icy bite to them. "I am not *yours*."

Her courage quickly deflated in the continued

force of his stare, and she turned her gaze from his.

Leanne shoulders sagged in relief when she saw Mike approaching to cut in.

"And now, the couple's first dance as husband and wife!" The emcee's voice reverberated in the ballroom as Mike's arms circled her waist. She felt the tension leave her body as she lost herself in Mike's steel gray gaze, his warm, appreciative smile, and the strength of his arms. Everything became a distant memory as Mike led Leanne around dance floor. She felt wrapped in his love, protected and secure.

He brushed an errant strand of hair from her forehead. "Do you remember when we first met?"

"It was the worst day of my life." At his horrified look, she giggled and shook her head. "No, I mean, it was until you came along."

He laughed. "For a second, you had me worried." His tone became husky as he continued. "You were standing by that heap of steaming junk you called a car, and you looked like you were about to cry."

"I think I would have cried if you hadn't come along when you did."

Mike kissed the top of her hair. "I love that I could rescue you." He twirled her around before adding, "I remember what you looked like. You were wearing that oversized sweatshirt you loved so much. I don't think I could even see your hands. Your jeans had an oil smudge on the thigh."

Leanne nodded, remembering feeling embarrassed when he pulled up next to her in the parking lot. The oil smudge was actually a stain from her lunch. Her stepfather had walked into the kitchen when he heard her mother yelling at her. "Go easy on her, Deborah, Lee-Lee is doing her best." Russell had defended her, coming to stand behind her and placing his hands on her shoulders. Leanne had murmured a quick excuse about needing to get back to class. In a rush to escape, she left her lunch on the table, and opted to grab a burger on the way to her next class, spilling on herself in the process. The sweatshirt happened to be in her backpack, and she had thrown it on in lieu of walking around with a big red and yellow stain on her chest.

Leanne had been counting the semesters until graduation, ready to escape her home. But her day – her life - had changed when Mike walked up to her that afternoon, the sun glistening off his golden brown hair, illuminating his finely chiseled features. She remembered thinking he was her picture-perfect dream of a knight in shining armor.

"You had your hair up in a ponytail." Mike continued where her memories left off. "But this one strand kept falling over your eyes." He bent his head, pressing his forehead lightly against hers. "Over the past year, I think I have tucked that hair back a hundred times." Brushing a gentle kiss on her forehead, he whispered. "And I can't wait to tuck it back a thousand more times, Mrs. McKinley."

Tears stung her eyes at his words. His love, his gentle assurances and sweet flattery, or even just a look from him across the room filled her heart so completely.

She whispered. "When can we leave?"

His words came out as a husky chuckle. "I'm eager to leave, too, but we have some things our guests are expecting us to do." Mike grinned in the face of her impatience. "Like cut the cake, toss the bouquet…"

"Well, can we hurry up and do them? I'm..." she pressed closer to him. "I just want to be alone with you."

His tender kiss bolstered her for the next half hour as they rushed through the rest of the reception.

As the two were preparing to leave, her mother found her way to Leanne's side. "You could have smiled when you were dancing with your father."

"Stepfather." Leanne mumbled, but then added firmly. "Mom, please stop criticizing everything."

"I'm not criticizing! For heaven's sake, Leanne, you are so sensitive. How did you come out so spineless? I'll never know! Neither of her sisters are so sensitive – then again, you aren't nearly successful as they are. Maybe if you weren't so touchy you wouldn't be heading off to your honeymoon with a mechanic."

Leanne growled out between clenched teeth, "Mike is a wonderful man."

Deborah was a woman who rarely showed any emotion other than disdain for others, but the barely leashed anger from her otherwise passive daughter caused a momentary flicker of astonishment to flicker across her face.

When she recovered, she raised an eyebrow and said, "Well, then you should consider yourself lucky that he is blind to all of your faults." Her mom turned on her heels, shaking her head, grumbling about Leanne's shortcomings along the way.

Mike appeared at her side and her hand sought his. As they ran to their car under a shower of rose petals and well wishes, Leanne was trailing behind her the dozen comments she had overhead her mother mutter to anyone who would listen, the pain from her past, and a secret or two she thought she could dispense of with a slam of their car door.

However, as the couple drove to their honeymoon suite at the Triple R Ranch and Resort, their hands sitting intertwined on the center console, Leanne found it wasn't quite so easy to shed her baggage. She watched the desert scenery whisk by as she tried to chase the tortured thoughts from her mind. *It doesn't matter; you are starting new, no more, no more, no more.* As the thoughts were whizzing through her head like the desert bushes which whipped past her view, she absentmindedly stroked her thumb across the back of Mike's hand.

"We have about an hour to go if you want to get some sleep." His thumb brushed the top of her hand, and she turned in the seat toward him.

"I can't possibly sleep." Leanne smiled at his handsome profile and let her thoughts have sound. "I can't believe you actually married me."

"You say that like you duped me into marrying you." Despite his teasing tone, a pang of guilt slammed into her happiness, causing her bright smile to fade a little.

"You have no idea how happy I am today, Leanne." After a moment he corrected himself. "No, how happy you have made me since you came into my life. I love your sweet and humble nature. I love how you are the peacemaker wherever we go, never stirring up strife, or causing problems. I can't wait until you are holding our children in your arms, imparting all these Godly characteristics to them." Mike shrugged and blushed a little as he stumbled through his compliment. "Being with you is like coming home after a long, hot day working on cars. After a day like that, you can't wait to step into the shower. I feel so refreshed and whole when I am with you."

She stirred a little in her seat. At her movement he asked. "Too mushy or too weird?"

"Neither." His words may have pricked her conscience, but she still loved to hear them. She never cared much about being Godly until he came along. He made her want to be good, despite her past. He made her want to be clean, despite the filth that covered her.

Mike's words pulled her out of her thoughts. "Leanne, you are so beautiful, inside and out."

Tears stung her eyes at the simple sweetness of his words. *God, please don't let him ever stop feeling this way about me!*

A half hour later, they arrived at the resort. Leanne stood in front of a strange-looking fountain situated in the middle of the lobby. The sign above the fountain said *The Firm Foundation Fountain*. Mike's parents had blessed them with the honeymoon trip as their wedding gift. "There is a lot you can learn there, and I think it is a great place to start your marriage." Mike's dad had said.

Mike came up behind her, slipping an arm about her waist. "Our room is upstairs." She felt his warm breath on her neck stirring her hair, and a shiver of anticipation crept up on her.

However, once inside their room, she felt a wave of shyness wash over her.

While Mike wasn't her first, she knew she was his. A wave of guilt washed over her at the lies she had already sown into the fabric of their relationship.

One night, while they were still dating, she had gotten carried away as she eagerly accepted his kisses. They were so sweet, so full of love, and she was desperate for them. She drank them as if they were water and she was dry, parched earth.

But her overzealous kissing had prompted him to stop her. "I think we need to stop, Leanne." Mike had said. At her perplexed and wounded look, he had asked, "Don't you?"

Caught, she had simply added another lie to the growing pile of deceit. "Of course."

There were some things better left unsaid, she reminded herself as she looked at her reflection in the hotel mirror. Like her mom always told her, she was blessed to find Mike. He didn't need to know anything about her past that had no bearing on their future. Now, she was free from her past, and Mike was her future.

She pressed a trembling hand to her stomach as she looked at her reflection. Her tall, lean body was clothed in a cream gown that was practically sheer, and her blonde hair tumbled loosely around her shoulders. Her eyes were large pools of ice blue in her all too pale face. Nonetheless, she looked like a beautiful temptress.

*Lee-Lee, you are too tempting to resist.*

Dashing away the tear that slipped down her cheek, she shoved aside her past and turned to head toward Mike.

"Leanne, you look so beautiful." Mike's voice was gruff with emotion.

*You make me feel beautiful inside.*

He stood before her, hesitant at first, then touching just the thin strap of her gown. "You look like the bride I've always imagined: beautiful, pure and sweet."

She looked down at his hand, which fluttered down her arm and over her waist. Leanne couldn't speak or look at him, lest her guilt be revealed.

When she didn't speak, he continued to heighten her guilt with his sweet compliments. "I like your gown."

It had been a gift from her sisters – her sisters who were smart, successful…untouched.

He misread her continued silence. Cupping her face in his calloused palms, he gently forced her to meet his steel-gray stare. The abundance of love she saw there made her chin quiver with a suppressed sob.

"Leanne, I am just as nervous as you are." His left thumb brushed her cheek, encountering a lone tear along the way. "But there is nothing to be ashamed of."

Shrugging aside her shame, she ran her hands up his muscular back. Her touch was barely a whisper of skin upon skin – she felt unworthy of his love, but she wanted to prove herself worthy of his tender gaze, his loving touch, and his sweet words.

She kissed him, trying to fight back the wave of tears that threatened to engulf her. The two tumbled to the bed, and she pulled him down for a kiss, drinking in his love. His kiss was full of sweet promises that washed away the bitter taste of her past. His hands touched her with tender passion, which incinerated the harsh life she had been raised under. And he whispered sweet endearments that bound up the tattered remains of her self-esteem.

She gasped when Mike pulled back to look down at her, fearing she had done something wrong, something to repulse him. Leanne breathed a sigh of relief when she didn't see anything but love in his eyes.

A tear traced a lonely path down her temple and into her golden hair. It was a tear mixed with joy and guilt, of unbelievable but undeserved happiness. Leanne cupped his face in her hands. "Thank you."

Leaning up on an elbow, Mike gazed down at her. His thumb – or maybe it was the look in his eyes –

dashed away her tear. A quizzical look came into his eyes. "For what?"

"For loving me."

He gently brushed her hair back. "Always."

# Chapter One

*Why doesn't he ever listen to me!*

Leanne tossed her purse into the passenger seat and was about to slide in when Mike came running up behind her.

"Honey, wait!" He was dangling the keys from his finger, a smirk playing about his handsome lips. "You weren't going to get very far without these."

Leanne wanted to snatch the keys from him, but her anger abated a little when he pulled her into his arms. The hot desert sun was directly behind him, illuminating the edges of his tawny hair. *He looks like a beautiful angel, complete with a halo,* she thought sardonically. Mike McKinley was the only man she knew that could spend all morning working on cars, yet look like he spent the day modeling coveralls for a Sear's catalogue.

Suddenly, his perfection stung.

"It's probably nothing. You know how Karen gets around new people." His words were meant to soothe her anxiety.

"I told you she wasn't ready." There was a resolute pout tucked in between Leanne's whispered syllables.

Ever since Karen, their oldest daughter, was born, Leanne had handled the books for the garage from home. However, Mike had spent the last year hounding her to come back to work with him, despite her protests that Karen wasn't going to do well in a daycare.

Mike gently hooked his forefinger under her chin, tilting her head upwards. His steel gaze imprisoned all of her protests, but she gladly surrendered to their bonds. "You can't hide her away from the world forever. Besides, she starts preschool next year." The firmness in his tone squelched her brief uprising, and she merely nodded. She wanted to argue, but the tender way he tucked her wayward blonde strand of hair behind her ear smothered any lingering protests.

She saw nothing but love in his tender gaze, and guilt crushed the argument that had started to bloom.

*I need his love.*

"I'll call you after I pick her up." Her promise came out as a defeated whisper.

In response, he brushed a brief kiss across her lips.

Backing out of his embrace, Leanne got in her car and drove off without even looking back at her husband.

The daycare was just a few blocks from the garage, and when Leanne parked her car in the parking lot, she drew a steadying breath before getting out.

The side of the building was painted in a colorful mural of children happily playing around the words *Little Angel's Childcare*. Several of the letters were drawn as playground equipment, and one of the cartoon children was sliding down the A.

From the call she received a few minutes ago, her daughter wasn't one of those happy children playing with gleeful abandon.

When she got inside, her gaze scanned the room for Karen. She spotted her rocking in the corner, rubbing her earlobe and sucking on her thumb between shuddering sobs. Before she could take a step toward her daughter, a voice stopped her.

"Mrs. McKinley, I'm sorry to have disturbed you, but we just couldn't console her." The daycare worker said as she came toward Leanne. The defensive apology was evident in the woman's voice.

"It is okay, Cathy. What happened?"

"She just kept walking around in circles saying the same thing over and over again." Leanne went over to Karen as the woman spoke. Cathy shrugged her shoulders, and Leanne turned to brush a damp golden curl off her daughter's forehead.

Leanne looked over her shoulder at Cathy as she continued. "But it didn't make any sense, Mrs. McKinley! Then she started screaming this awful scream, and..."

Leanne saw the look on Cathy's face: frustration and worthlessness, mingled with love. Leanne knew that feeling all too well.

"What was she saying?" Leanne asked.

"She kept whispering, 'What do you want? How do you ask for it?'" Cathy shrugged and added, "She was fine before that. We had just come from outside, and the kids were all getting ready for snack time."

Understanding dawned on Leanne and she sighed. "She says that when she wants something. It is sort of like an echo of what I would say to her. She does it when she's upset or anxious in a situation."

Cathy's blank look elicited another weary sigh from Leanne. "If she wants some juice and comes up and points to it, I asked her, "What do you want? How do you ask for it?" Dawning came slowly to the worker and then she chuckled. "Oh, that's so cute."

*Yeah, except when you come in and find your daughter sobbing in the corner because she can't communicate a basic need to you. In her eyes, she thinks she is conveying what she wants, but you aren't understanding.* She would have loved to scream this at the top of her lungs for the whole daycare to hear, but Leanne simply nodded. It was easier to take care of Karen on her own, rather than to try to explain to everyone.

"I'm sorry, I..." Leanne didn't know how to finish her sentence. But she didn't have to, because the daycare worker spoke up.

"No, I'm sorry I couldn't help her. She was so worked up and started rocking in the corner, rubbing her ears. But anything I did to console her seemed to make it worse."

"Thank you, Cathy." Leanne meant it sincerely, but she wasn't sure her voice conveyed that. All Leanne wanted to do was go home with her children. *And hide from everyone?* The self-criticism scampered across her mind like a malicious imp.

Turning to Karen, she said, "Let's get your brother and go home, baby." Karen grabbed her mom's hand, still rubbing her earlobe in agitation. Picking up the girl's brand new backpack, the two started toward the toddler room, both of their shoulders drooping in defeat.

Like it or not, Mike was just going to have to accept the fact that this wasn't going to work right now. She could still do the accounting and office work from home. *Please don't let him be disappointed in me. I need him.*

"Mrs. McKinley, might I have a moment?"

Leanne turned toward Mrs. Henley, the owner of the daycare. The last thing she wanted was a lecture from this woman about bringing her rowdy daughter to the center. With her head hung down, Leanne followed the woman into her office until she felt the tug on her arm.

"Come on, baby, let's go home." Karen's words came out as a question and her face was etched with confusion.

Mrs. Henley bent down to Karen. "I have some books that I know you're fond of. Would you like to read those while I talk to your mommy?" Without making eye contact with the woman, Karen followed the woman's direction. After several furtive glances at Leanne, she settled down in a bean bag to read.

"I am sorry for the trouble today, Mrs. Henley." Leanne began, wanting to get this admonishment over with.

The woman shook her head at Leanne's words. "There is no need to apologize, and please call me Angel." After settling herself behind the desk, she laced her fingers together and rested her forearms on the top of the immaculate desk. "I wanted to talk with you about some of the things I noticed this week with Karen, and some accommodations we can make here in the classroom to make her learning experience the best it can be."

"Accommodations?"

"I've noticed some areas of concern - some possible developmental delays."

Leanne's brows furrowed in confusion. "Delays? Delays in what?"

"For instance, her communication. Have you brought that up to her doctor?"

"Dr. Meston said she's fine. He's amazed she can read. He's heard her speak, but he said let's just wait and see if things improve when she gets in school. It's only been a week." Leanne's excuses came out like a shotgun blast, each one aimed at the woman's comments and spreading out over a wide area. Gathering her things, she added. "Besides, this doesn't even matter; she won't be coming back here. You don't have to worry about her disrupting classes again." Leanne felt the tears stinging the back of her eyes. She didn't want to stay a moment longer for fear that the tears would burst from her eyes in front of this put-together, confidant woman, with her immaculately clean desk, and clutter free office.

The woman stood and reached across the desk, lightly holding Leanne's hand. "Mrs. McKinley, Karen is a beautiful child and I want her to continue on here. I believe the early intervention we can provide will help her. The school system has a great special education program for early intervention, and through us, we can get the ball rolling on testing."

Leanne sat back in the chair, wishing Mike was here. A thousand choice words popped into her head, but the scathing retort dwindled to apologetic excuses by time they hit her lips. "I know she can be a bit quirky, but special education?" Leanne shook her head. "I think she's fine...she's not slow. She's very bright and she can read. She's only four and she can read. Did you know that?"

Leanne didn't miss the look of pity the woman gave her. "Karen is *very* bright!" Mrs. Henley assured her, but Leanne wondered if it was sincere. After all, hadn't she just said her daughter was behind developmentally? Why couldn't Mike be here?

The woman handed her a packet of information. "Why don't you take these? You and your husband can look it over, and we can all sit down and talk about what educational approach is best for Karen."

Leanne nodded as she stood up. "Let's go Karen."

After picking up Rick from the toddler room, the three headed out to the parking lot.

Once in the car, she pulled out her phone to call Mike, but tossed it on the seat next to her. She didn't want to hear him shrug off her concerns, or brush away her tears with his placating, "It's going to be okay, honey."

Tears rolled down her face as she thought about what Mrs. Henley had said. Maybe the woman had a point. Karen did show a few differences from the other kids at the church daycare.

When Karen started going to the nursery at

church, Leanne had seen a subtle dissimilarity between Karen and the other kids. When Leanne had tried to talk to Mike about it, he would always brushed aside her concerns. "You need to get her out with other kids more!" The argument was all too familiar, but it was one she had never pushed too hard against.

Leanne gnawed on her fingernail. Maybe she should be more adamant about getting her daughter help. But Mike's love was more like a pat on the head these days. All she needed was to push him farther away and she would lose him.

Leanne cranked up the car and headed for home. As soon as the car rumbled to a start, the radio came on. Karen began singing the words to the children's Bible song CD that was playing. It was Karen's favorite and they listened to little else in the car.

Leanne glanced at her daughter in the rearview mirror. Though her brow was furrowed, Karen sang as if the afternoon hadn't been filled with tearful screams and outbursts. Leanne couldn't help but let out a teary laugh when her daughter belted out in a robust voice, "Standing in the peanut bread!" instead of "standing in the need of prayer."

Dashing the tears from her cheeks, she tried to shrug aside the daycare director's words, but they stuck with her all the way home.

Once they got to the house, Karen ran directly to her room. Rick brought Leanne a couple of books to read, rubbing his eyes as if he could dash the sleep from them. His chubby cheeks dimpled in a smile, and she hauled him into her lap as she sat on the couch. He was asleep before she finished reading the second book, and she carried him to his room.

After closing Rick's door, she peeked in at Karen, and found her on the floor of her room, lining up her Little People toys and singing a song. It was one of the things she brought up to Mike often. She never actually played with the toys; she lined them up, examined them and spun them in her hands.

As usual, he dismissed her concerns. She knew he meant well - that he wanted to ease her fears, but she wished he would just listen to her.

*Maybe he can't stomach the idea of anything being less than perfect.*

She chased the thought away as quickly as it came. Mike was loving and forgiving – he'd never…

*But then why do you hide your past?*

In an effort to escape her intrusive and bullying thoughts, she sat down with Karen on the floor. The girl gave her a brief glance before turning back to her toys, still singing.

"What's his name?" Leanne asked, pointing to one of the figures.

"Eddie." Karen's reply was short, followed by more singing.

"Where's his frog?"

Karen merely pointed to the frog without ceasing her rocking and singing.

After several failed attempts to draw her into conversation, Leanne left her daughter to play and soothe herself.

Walking out to the kitchen, Leanne picked up the phone to call Mike, but hung up before even punching in his number.

She sat on the kitchen stool and rested her head in her hands. Her eyes fell on the information packet that Mrs. Henley gave her.

She used her fingers to spread the brochures out, reading their titles with a heavy heart. *Developmental Milestones*, *Autism Spectrum Disorders*, *A Parent's Guide to Special Education*. She flipped through the *Autism Spectrum Disorders* brochure.

Leanne sat up a little straighter in the chair as she read the pamphlet. As she read through the bulleted list under the heading **What are some of the signs of ASDs**, she alternately dismissed her concerns and then hesitantly took them up again. Sure Karen had trouble expressing her needs and she echoed words and phrases, but that was only when she was upset. At the same time, Karen didn't mind being held and she was aware when other people spoke to her. But the more Leanne read, the more she began seeing her daughter's behavior.

Mike's voice rang through her head. *We all have our quirks. Don't read into her behavior.*

She thought of calling Mike again, but dialed her sister's number instead. She knew there would be consequences for her actions; her mom would eventually find out.

"Hey, Loretta, sorry to bother you." Why did she feel like all her sentences began with an apology?

"Sis, you are never bothering me. I miss you. You hardly ever call."

"Sorry." *There I go again,* she thought. "It has been crazy around here. That's why I called." Leanne explained everything that Mrs. Henley said, plus her own concerns, throwing in Mike's excuses - just in case she was overreacting.

*Mom and Mike would say I am overdramatizing and overanalyzing everything.*

"Oh, Leanne." The concern for her sister and her niece was evident in Loretta's voice. "You should have called me earlier. How is she doing now?"

"She's calm and playing in her room."

"And you? How are you and Mike handling all of this?"

"Fine, just trying to make sense out of all the information being thrown at me."

Loretta, the sister and aunt, was replaced by Dr. Loretta McLain, Director of Early Childhood Education in her district. "I can tell you that Mrs. Henley was doing her job, so try not to be upset with her. It is her responsibility to bring any concerns she sees to the parents' attention. However, I would definitely talk with Karen's pediatrician."

An argument whispered across her mind and she echoed it before it skittered away. "We *have* brought the communication issue up with Dr. Meston before. He said we should wait and see how she adapts when she starts school."

Loretta paused for a moment and the silence that stretched between them deflated Leanne's argument.

Finally, Loretta spoke. "Well, didn't she start school? Didn't the director point out concerns?"

Loretta's questions made Leanne's motherly judgments feel insignificant – she began second guessing everything again.

"Yes," Leanne bit her nail before she continued. "But special education! Mike is going to have a fit!"

"Karen does sound like she has more than a few red flags to warrant testing."

Leanne brushed the tears from her eyes, hoping her sister could not hear them through her voice. "Okay."

"And, Leanne, it is just testing. It is better to know for sure either way."

After she hung up, she let her tears have full reign. She couldn't escape the feeling that her daughter's problems were her fault. Leanne had difficulty during both of her pregnancies. She had always wondered if it had to do with her past, but she had never disclosed the information to her doctor. Guilt assailed her – she knew she should have said something to the doctor. However, Hamilton was a small town, and Nathan, Mike's young brother, taught Dr. Meston's son. What if Mike found out? He would be disgusted and leave her. She needed him.

*God, please make this nightmare go away!* She cringed at the prayer she had whispered daily when she was eighteen. God had answered her prayer, but was she now paying the consequences for it?

*You are not fit to be a mother!*

The phone interrupted her abusive thoughts.

Glancing at the caller ID, she was ashamedly relieved it wasn't Mike. "Loretta just called and told me!" Lacey's voice sounded reproachful. Her older sister was tough, blunt, and to the point – not unlike their mother. But where Deborah's brusque comments were spiteful, Lacey's were filled with love and a compassionate truth meant to help you, not designed to belittle you.

"I love you." Leanne knew this was a precursor to a forthright comment about her deficiencies. "But, Leanne, this isn't something you can sit on the fence about. You've never been much of a fighter. You always just sat around and let life happen to you."

Tears stung Leanne's eyes at the hurtful truth of her sister's words, wondering if her sister knew more about her past.

"This is your daughter, Leanne. If you want her to be successful, you are going to have to fight for her. You have *always* settled for whatever came your way. But don't just settle when it comes to your daughter, okay?"

Lacey's words were like a pick axe chipping away at her heart. However, there were little nuggets of wisdom tucked between the barbs, and they stung her conscience.

# Chapter Two

"Why didn't you call me?" Mike said when he came through the door later that evening.

Leanne shrugged and continued cutting the vegetables for dinner. "I was drained. Besides, I called Loretta for some advice, and then Lacey called, and..."

Mike took the knife from her hands and folded her in his arms. *Like a hug is going to make all this go away!* But she knew her inner blustering had no teeth. Mike's hugs always bolstered her strength. Though it never seemed like it was enough lately, she would settle for what he gave now.

"So tell me what happened."

Leanne related all that Mrs. Henley and her sister had said.

Mike's head jerked back and roared. "Special education!"

Leanne knew that would be Mike's reaction, and she closed her eyes at his objections. "There is nothing wrong with her. She just needs a little more structure and a little more socialization."

She put both hands on his chest and looked away for a moment, gathering the courage to say what was on her mind. *Please don't let him be upset.*

Leanne drew a deep breath, as if more oxygen in her lungs would give her more courage. "Her hair was wet and matted from both her tears and her sweat. She had scratches on her arms, and the look in her eyes was so tortured." Tears pooled in Leanne's crystal blue eyes. "This is not a discipline problem, Mike. This is not something a simple hug is going to fix."

Mike took a step back for a moment. He stared down at her as if trying to gauge her emotions. She had stood her ground, all the while fearing his reaction. The freedom of voicing her objections mingled with guilt and dread, but she tried her best to sound firm. "I think we should start with Dr. Meston."

Mike turned his head as if to say no, but Leanne was shocked when it only came out as a hesitant, "I don't know."

He cupped her face in his hands, brushing his thumbs across her cheeks. "I wonder if it isn't because she's just a little sensitive. She wears her emotions on her sleeve - like you. So when someone brushes against it, you get hurt."

His gestures were so gentle, but his words cut her heart. Maybe that just proved his point.

"But if it will set your mind at ease, we will take her in."

With a brief kiss on the top of her head, he walked down the hall. "I'm going to get cleaned up for dinner." Mike tossed over his shoulder.

Leanne watched his retreating back. She wanted to count this as a victory, but his conciliatory gestures rubbed at her wrong. *Weary love* – the words whispered across her mind. She thought they were a perfect description of her husband's attitude toward her lately.

She brooded silently throughout dinner, wondering what she could do to change the way things were going in their marriage. Leanne glanced at him across the table. He was perfect. His golden brown hair was always closely cropped, not a hair out of place. His finely chiseled jawline never held the hint of stubble. Even his nails were pristine. *He's a mechanic!* Leanne shouted in her mind. *His nails should carry at least a trace of grease.*

Leanne tucked an errant strand of her blond hair behind her ear. *And here I am, the farthest thing from perfect.*

Mike caught her staring at him and flashed her a quick smile. It was warm, friendly, and sweet.

Concern knitted her brow. *Maybe he is bored and wants to leave me.* His goodbye morning kisses used to hold sizzling promises for his return home. His "I'm home from work" kisses used to make her count down the minutes until the kids would go to bed. Now they seemed like obligatory chores of a marriage grown cold.

Leanne fiddled with the napkin in her lap. Maybe she would have to do something about that tonight.

*Lee-Lee*

The whispered nickname haunted her mind, but she chased it away with an inward cry. *This is different. This is pure.*

Later that evening, Leanne sat with Karen in her room. Karen's Little People toys were still lined up across one of her books. "What are you playing?"

Karen picked up one of the figures. "Michael

loves to paint and draw, and he can make magical things happen with his drawings." The girl went on to explain each of the characters in detail, and Leanne wondered at the legitimacy of her earlier concerns. Maybe Mike was right. She can speak so well, she was extremely smart, and it was only when she was upset that she echoed people's words. But as Karen continued, Leanne began to recognize Karen's explanation of the characters were a carbon copy from one of her books.

"It's your mom." Mike startled her as he came into the room, handing her the phone. Rick came charging in behind him, scattering the carefully lined toys in the process.

The disruption of her toys caused Karen to begin screaming the words to the Little People song. Her words came out in terrified grunts. "I got this." Mike said, and shooed her out of the room. She looked indecisively at the phone. The last thing she needed right now was a lecture from her mom, but Mike firmly pushed her out the door. "You have a nice chat with your mom. I can handle this."

It was hard to walk away from Karen, who was rocking back and forth singing the Little People song in a grunting and growling voice.

"What in the world is going on over there?" Her mom said when she finally put her ear to the phone.

"Karen is just a little upset right now." Leanne wanted the conversation to end and it had barely started. "What do you need?"

"I don't need anything. I have to have a reason to

call my daughter and check up on her?"

"No, Mom."

"Lacey called and told me what happened today."

*Of course she did.* Leanne rolled her eyes. Conversations with her mother over the phone were easier because she could at least make faces to voice her frustration.

"You need to listen to your sister and get her tested."

"I know, Mom. Mike and I have already discussed it."

"There is obviously something wrong with her." Her mom clicked her tongue in reproach. "I wish I had gotten *you* tested when you were little. But back then, we didn't know the things that they know now."

"Me?" As soon as the question left her lips, Leanne wished she hadn't asked.

"You were always so moody. Especially after your father died and Russell came to live with us." After a thoughtful pause, her mom continued her verbal assault, oblivious to the pain she was inflicting. "You know, if I remember correctly, I think there's something on your dad's side of the family. You know you always took after your dad while your sisters took after me."

*Of course*, Leanne thought, *because they are successful, smart and wonderful.*

"Look, I need to go mom." That was the other great thing about phone conversations with her mother; she could invent excuses to hang up.

"Wait, dear."

Leanne despised *dear* when it tumbled from her mother's lips. "What, Mom?"

"Russell and I were talking, and we think you might need a break. You and Mike need to get away for a while. We want to take the kids for a..."

"No!" The word exploded from her lips before she could temper it. "I mean, I don't think that would be good for Karen right now. Look mom, I need to go."

She hung up on her mother's protests. Deborah had said fight for her daughter, and that is one issue she would fight to the death over. There would *never* be a time when Karen or Rick spent one night in that house.

Placing a hand on her chest to still her racing heart, it slowly dawned on her that the house was silent. Walking down the hall, she peeked in to find Rick curled up on his bed, sound asleep. She kissed the top of his tawny hair and pulled the covers up. Her steps faltered as she walked into Karen's room. The two had fallen asleep in the rocking chair, Mike's head resting on top of Karen's. She had her thumb in her mouth and her other hand rested on Mike's arm. Every once in a while, her body would shudder, a left over tremor from the violence of her cries.

Leanne leaned against the doorway and smiled. A memory of when Karen was a baby trickled back to her. Karen had fallen asleep on Mike's chest, and when he moved a fraction of an inch, she had howled in protest. "I'm sorry, little princess." Mike had said.

When Mike had settled Karen in her crib, Leanne had come up behind him and wrapped her arms around his waist. "She's got you wrapped around her little chubby finger."

"Just like her mommy." His husky reply had sent a shiver of excitement through her.

Leanne's smile faded with the memory. She missed that Mike - the one who was always teasing her, kissing her, passionately loving her. Now it felt like all his kisses were only conciliatory reassurances of his love.

She wanted to kiss him awake, something she had done when they were first married. It had never failed to bring a sleepy, but saucy, smile to his handsome face.

She bent down to brush her lips against his, but thought better of it. It had been awhile since she had elicited a response like that from him – what if he rejected her?

She lightly touched his face, laying a hand along his chiseled jaw line. His steel grey eyes slowly opened, and a soft smile touched his lips at the sight of her. Before she could stop herself, she bent down and kissed him, careful not to wake Karen.

The moment was brief, a whisper among kisses, but she saw the corner of his lip lift in a smirk.

"Let me get her in bed." He mouthed.

They took turns kissing Karen goodnight once they had her tucked in bed. Mike loosely held Leanne's hand as they walked down to their room. The gentle intimacies they once shared, like holding hands or snuggling on the couch, were shelved over the past six years. The first two years were a fiery inferno, but slowly, she had seen the fire dwindle to a smoldering heap of a marriage.

Once inside their room, she drew him close to her. He arched an eyebrow, but his lips soon captured hers. She leaned up on her toes, eager for his love, his passion, his desire. His love was like water washing over her, cleansing her, filling her up. She tried to put that same love back into her kisses - her touch. But her heart was so filled with holes that, like a sieve, she fruitlessly fought to hold on to his love, let alone return it.

She felt Mike's desire was present but detached, and with her hands, body and lips she tried to perform surgery on their marriage. Despite his distance and distraction, she reached for the buttons on his shirt, hoping to push past it, but his hands reached for hers, stilling her progress.

Sitting down on the edge of their bed, he gathered her close until she stood between his outstretched legs. He rested his forehead against her stomach, and she laced her fingers through his sandy brown hair.

This wasn't intimacy and romance. There was weariness and defeat in his movements, and they were confirmed by his words. "I've never seen her so worked up." When Mike finally looked up at her, there were unshed tears glimmering in his steel gray eyes. "I'm scared because I don't know how to fix this."

Her disappointment at their loss of a romantic moment fled in the face of his tears. Cupping his cheeks, she said nothing because she didn't know what to say. She didn't know what was wrong with Karen, let alone how they could fix it.

Mike took one of his hands off her hips and swiped his eyes. "I'm sorry."

He pulled her down to the bed with him, and she rested her head on his chest. He absentmindedly played with her golden tresses, while she fiddled with the buttons on his shirt. Leanne wanted...no, needed the intimacy that had been kindling before. But with a weary resignation, she knew they were miles away from the passion they had briefly shared.

He rolled both of them onto their side so the two were facing each other. "So, what did your mother have to say?"

Their bodies were just a breath away from each other, and she wanted to feel a tangible evidence of his love, an outward sign of his affection. The conversation with her mother was the last thing she wanted to discuss.

She rolled onto her back. A shadow crossed her features. "Lacey told her about our conversation, and my mom said we need to have her tested."

Leanne would have got up, but Mike pulled her back down. "No, that's not it."

"It's just her usual belittling comments. They just got to me."

Mike's steely gaze bore into her. She looked away, but her face must have betrayed her guilt.

"I see that look on your face; something more than your mother's usual barbs happened."

She wanted to end this conversation before they

got into dangerous waters. Trying to distract him, she ran her hand inside the open collar of his shirt, up the back of his neck, and threaded her fingers into the nape of his hair. She offered her lips up for a kiss, but they were only met with his breath as he whispered her name. Leanne opened her eyes, for the whisper was not a husky whisper of desire, but a stern warning.

Letting her hand fall to the bed next to her, she shrugged and tried to sound nonchalant. "My mom and Russell asked to take the kids for a weekend."

Mike's expression meant that she better get out her life preserver, because the dangerous waters she was so desperately trying to avoid were up ahead - and they were going in.

He arched an eyebrow in confusion. "Well, would that be so bad?"

"No!" Pulling herself out from under him, she got off the bed and stormed over to the dresser. She yanked out her nightgown and looked at him in the mirror as he came up behind her. "I told you when we had her, she would never spend any time alone with them."

"Leanne, I know your mother can be harsh, but..."

She spun around. "You promised."

She didn't even realize that she was crying until Mike brushed the tear from her cheek. "Okay." He pulled her in for a hug, but she pushed away. The intimacy was gone and she slammed the bathroom door to change for bed.

By the time she donned her nightgown and

brushed her teeth, her anger had abated. In its place was regret and guilt.

When she emerged from the bathroom, she found Mike sitting on the bed, looking as stunned as he had when she stormed off.

"I'm sorry." She came to kneel before him. "I shouldn't have been so angry."

She placed her hands lightly on his thighs, looking up into his steel gray eyes beseechingly. He cupped her face and bent down to brush her lips lightly with his.

With a heart to please, she sought to show him how sorry she was. He pulled back from their kiss, an unnamed emotion wreaking havoc in his eyes. "Leanne," Mike began.

Leanne wasn't about to be deterred; she would make amends for her outburst. Like the buttons on his shirt, one by one she silently dispensed with the objections and reservations she saw in his eyes and she felt in his touch.

"Leanne, you don't need to..."

She cut off his words. "Please, Mike. I love you."

"I know you do." His words came out one by one as she feathered kisses across his face. But with a skill she learned all too early, she obliterated the rest of his sentence. Her body, her love, was an offering to him, and if he rejected it, he rejected her.

When he cried out his love for her, she drank it in, like a thirsty wanderer in the desert who had found a secret oasis. And if it disappeared in the morning, she didn't care. Right now, she was basking in the cool water of his love.

# Chapter Three

"Come on in, Son." Andrew McKinley clapped Mike on the back in a hug and then turned to embrace Leanne.

"How are you feeling, Dad?"

"Blessed to have all my children and my two grandchildren in the house tonight."

Mike smiled, but worry knit his brow. His father's health hadn't improved much, even with his younger brother, Nathan, stepping in to take over the senior pastor position at the church.

"Grandma!" Rick squealed and took off toward the kitchen after giving Andrew a hug and a kiss.

"How are you doing?" Andrew asked as he scooped up Karen. She looked at him for a moment, and then laid her head on his shoulder rather than answering.

Placing a weathered hand on his granddaughter's back, Andrew kissed the top of her golden curls. As if he understood the offering of her silent embrace, he whispered, "I love you, too, Karen."

The moment was interrupted by the sound of laughter coming from the kitchen. Moments later, Nathan, Mike's younger brother, and his fiancé, Kristina, came toward them.

"Rick came running into the kitchen calling for Mom." Nathan's explanation was littered with laughter. "The second she picked him up, he leaned over and swiped a cookie."

Mike chuckled. "Sounds like Rick - using a hug as a carefully devised maneuver to obtain a cookie."

"Nonsense!" Sandra McKinley said as she emerged from the kitchen with Rick in her arms. There were two dollops of chocolate nesting in the dimples of his wide grin. "He loves his grandma just as much as he loves his cookies."

As if to prove her correct, Rick kissed Sandra's cheek, transferring some of the chocolate in the process.

When Sandra set Rick down and headed back to the kitchen to finish with dinner, Nathan pulled Mike to the side.

"Mike," Nathan began, "you know I want you by my side as my best man when Kristina and I get married."

"Have you two set the date?"

Nathan nodded. "We are going to announce it at dinner tonight."

Mike clapped his brother on the back in a warm hug. "I'm happy for you, Nate." Stepping back, Mike added, "I knew when she came storming into my garage, shooting icy glares at you, that the two of you would end up together."

"You did not!" Nathan protested.

"She got under your skin that very first day, and you couldn't shake her from your mind." Mike's gaze sought out Leanne as she stood across the room, laughing with Kristina. That is how Mike had felt for Leanne when he first saw her at college. But now...

He scattered his objections before they had a

voice. But throughout dinner, Mike watched Nathan and Kristina. Kristina would say something and then lay her hand along Nathan's arm, or lean into him when she laughed.

It wasn't that Mike and Leanne's marriage lacked physicality. A blush stained his cheekbones as he thought about their lovemaking last night. As passionate as it was, there was something missing – something off with the way she touched him. He missed Leanne's simple touch, he missed her carefree laugh, and he missed waking up with her snuggled in his arms.

*Don't long for what you don't have! That's how marriages get in trouble!* The warning went off in his head. His friend had ruined his marriage with an affair that began when the man started complaining about what his wife wasn't. It didn't take long before he had found someone who fulfilled all those things. It wasn't until the man's marriage was ruined that he realized all that he did have with his wife.

Mike shook his own misgivings aside and tried to settle his expectations on the blessings before him. He looked at his wife, and she smiled at something Kristina was saying to her. Leanne was still as beautiful as ever, her long ash blond hair up in its usual ponytail. Sometimes he longed to hide all her ponytail holders and plastic hair clips so she was forced to leave her golden tresses down. As if feeling his eyes upon her, Leanne turned her ice blue gaze upon him. For a brief moment, a furrow knitted her brow. She smiled tentatively at first, but when he covered her hand with his, the smile warmed and blossomed. She interlaced her fingers with his and leaned a little toward him.

"Is something wrong?" She whispered.

"No, I was just thinking you look beautiful." A blush stained his wife's cheeks, and if the room hadn't been filled with his family, he might have kissed her until her cheeks were flaming hot. The corner of his lips lifted in a saucy smirk as he thought about doing it anyway.

As if she could read his thoughts, his wife's blush got the slightest shade darker.

Nathan cleared his throat, breaking the spell that was holding them. "We asked you all to come to dinner here tonight, because Kristina and I have an announcement." Nathan smiled down at Kristina before proceeding. "We have set a date for our wedding, and we've decided to get married in April."

The table erupted with applause and booming well-wishes.

His mother and Kristina began excitedly discussing the wedding planning.

"We need to go dress shopping immediately!" His mom cried out, followed by Kristina's insistence that one of her former students join them. "That is if Barbara can make it. She's due any day."

"All the more reason we hustle this along!" His mom exclaimed.

At the same time, Mike had risen from the table and was clapping his brother on the back. As he was booming out his congratulations, Mike caught sight of

Karen at the table with her hands over her ears, a stricken look on her face.

His dad reached Karen before Leanne or he could get to the tormented girl. "Karen, can you help me get the plates ready for desert?"

"Me too!" Rick exclaimed, jumping up to follow. Mike swooped him up and said, "Not so fast there. I need you to help me congratulate your Uncle Nate!"

Mike laughed at his son's obvious disappointment in job assignments. The boy would have preferred to be involved with the whip cream and pie action in the kitchen.

As Mike watched his dad take Karen by the hand and lead her into the kitchen, with a fretful Leanne following in their wake, Mike sighed wearily. If it wasn't his daughter reacting violently to everything around her, it was his wife, crumbling before him. Tucking his disappointment aside, he turned back to the engaged couple.

"Mike," Nathan said, pulling Kristina close to his side. Nathan smiled down at her warmly before turning back to his brother. "Kristina and I want to have Rick and Karen in the ceremony as well."

Touched by his brother's gesture, he said, "Sure, little brother. That would be great."

Unbeknownst to him, this really wasn't such a great idea, at least in Leanne's eyes.

On the short drive home, Leanne turned to him with a smile. "Did you know Kristina asked me to be one of her bridesmaids?"

"I had a feeling she would. Nate asked me to be

his best man."

Her delicate eyebrows came together in a worried frown. "Oh, I hadn't thought about who would sit with Karen and Rick if we are both in the ceremony."

"Didn't Kristina tell you that they want Rick to be the ring bearer and Karen to be the flower girl?"

Silence filled the car for a few moments. "I don't know..."

"Come on, Leanne. Everything is going to be fine."

Leanne crossed her arms and looked out the window, while Mike tapped the steering wheel to the song on the stereo, oblivious to her stormy mood.

Even with Karen's reaction, tonight had been wonderful. He thought about the brief moment of intimacy him and Leanne had shared at the table. It felt wonderful to feel her hand in his, to see her blush and smile. He missed the love they used to share. He knew she was always so tired, and after the kids were asleep, she would head off to their room and he'd stay down in the living room watching TV so as not to disturb her.

But he had decided he was wrong to just settle for what they had. Tonight, he was going to try and rekindle the effortless love and sincerity that had died in their relationship, and he was going to press her to take her parents up on their offer.

When they pulled up in the driveway, Mike leaned across the center console and kissed her briefly, smirking at Rick and Karen's giggle. "I'll put the kids to bed."

He let the suggestion hang between their lips for a moment, and then hopped out of the car, unbuckling the kids from their car seats and scooting them off to get ready for bed.

After baths, stories and sleepy kisses, Mike walked into the master bedroom to find Leanne sitting up in bed. He smiled as he crawled across the bed, kissing her on her cheek.

She looked so beautiful with her blonde hair loose around her shoulders. She had a long, graceful neck that reminded him of a ballerina. He crouched on all fours next to her on the bed, placing a kiss along the slim column of her neck.

She laid a hand along his cheek, but Mike could see the concern in her eyes.

With a weary sag to his shoulders, he reluctantly asked her what was wrong.

"I'm worried about Karen."

"Let's wait and see what Dr. Meston has to say." He placed more kisses along her neck, thinking the matter over.

"No, I don't mean that." She placed a hand lightly on his chest, stilling his actions. "Did you not see how she reacted tonight when everyone got a little loud? How do you think she is going to handle walking up with a church full of people?"

With a sigh, Mike sat back on his heels. "She is going to do fine, and we can walk her through it. Like we did when we were getting her ready for the daycare." The example was out of his mouth before he realized the stupidity in his words. That certainly wasn't going to ease her mind.

"Well, that turned out well." The sarcasm that dripped from her tongue caused Mike to jerk his head back in surprise. This was not the soft-spoken Leanne he was used to.

"It's not like we are asking her to walk down a football field in the midst of a game. The wedding guests aren't going to be whooping and hollering." Mike joked, expecting a giggle. Instead, he was met with her angry glare and crossed arms. Her ice blue eyes were flashing fire at his offhanded joke.

"She will freak out about the sounds, the lights, and the change."

Mike sighed, all thoughts of cuddling smothered by her anger.

"Or are you just going to ignore it like you do everything else?"

Her accusation stung, and the frustration that had been silently bubbling underneath now boiled over. "I'm the one ignoring?" Mike boomed. "You have spent the past few years ignoring life!"

Her mouth hung open in astonishment. She turned her head away from him, but not before he saw her lip tremble with suppressed tears.

He tried to gentle his tone, but he didn't realize how good it felt to get those words out. "You have been avoiding everything: work, taking the kids to the daycare - you don't even take Karen to the grocery store anymore!"

"She doesn't like all the sounds..."

Mike jumped off the bed and walked toward the

bathroom, but thought better of it. Whirling around, he exploded. "Enough with the excuses!" He ran a hand across his face in frustration and came to stand by her side of the bed.

She finally met his gaze, and the wounded look on her face caused him to gentle his tone. "I'm not saying there isn't anything wrong with her, but whatever is going on with her, you can't use it as an excuse to hide her away."

"I'm not trying to hide her away." Her voice was a panic-stricken whisper, sending a dose of guilt his way for using such a sharp tone.

Leanne continued, her chin quivering as she spoke. "You don't have to see the look on her face everyday, the struggles that she has day in and day out."

He sat down near her hip, gently gripping her arms. "No, I don't. And I have tried to come home and be supportive. I've tried to take some of that emotional burden off you. But it's like you don't want to give it up."

He saw the tears pool in her eyes, and he laid his hand along her cheek. "Leanne, I love you and I want our marriage back. I want my wife back."

"But last night I…" Confusion knit her brow, but Leanne let her words trail off, shaking her head before she continued. "I haven't gone anywhere."

"I think we both have. I think we are settling for less than what God intended for our marriage." Confusion flickered in the depth of her ice blue eyes. "I miss coming home and snuggling on the couch with you, holding hands in church, kissing you right here..." he placed a kiss along her neck, eliciting a giggle from her. "...while you are cooking dinner, knowing I'm lighting a spark that is going to smolder until the kids go to bed."

Leanne placed her forehead against his, cupping his jaw in her hand. "I miss that, too."

"Then let's get it back. Let's take some time off together, just you and me." She laid back in the bed, bringing his head down for a kiss.

"Like right now?" The sultry tone in her voice elicited a smirk, and he chuckled,

"Yes, now. But let's also get away for the weekend. Let's take your parents up on their offer."

Whatever else he had planned to say was incinerated in the fury of her next words. "How dare you bring that up?" She shoved hard on his chest, rolling out from under him and off the bed. Crossing her arms, she whirled around and faced him. He couldn't believe the fierceness of her response and the tears that were streaming down her face.

Walking over to her, he reached out to touch her, but she took a step back. "You promised me the other night, and you promised me when we got married - our children would never set foot in that house. My daughter will never be alone with him."

Mike stood in the middle of their bedroom, confusion causing him to cock his head to the side, his eyebrows drawn together. "Russell? Are you talking about your stepfather?"

Leanne seemed to be trying to control her labored

breathing. "You promised me. I trusted you!"

"Leanne," Mike began, stunned by the force of her anger. "I'm sorry for even bringing it up. I didn't know…"

"No, you don't!" She stormed out of the room, leaving Mike wondering what just happened.

# Chapter Four

Mike and Leanne's argument from the night before weighed heavy on Mike all day. He had gone after her last night, only to find her locked in the office. He could hear her sobs from the other side of the door, but his requests for her to open it and talk to him went unanswered. She had finally come to bed around midnight, but she slipped under the covers without a word. Each had their backs turned, hugging the edge of the mattress, an icy space between them. They may have slept, but he doubted that either one got any rest. They woke up the next morning in the same stiff, unforgiving position. He rolled over, wanting to put an end to the silence, but she stiffened at his touch and sprang toward the bathroom before he had a chance to speak.

The sound of crackling bacon and the gurgle of the coffee pot was all that met his ears at breakfast. He never left the house without kissing his wife on the cheek, but the firm, thin line of her lips as she worked in the kitchen told him that today, his lips would be lonely. He settled for a quick kiss against the top of his children's sleepy heads as they padded past him to the breakfast table.

Now, he sat in the office at the garage, staring blindly at the computer screen. He was supposed to be ordering a part for May Williams' car. He shook his thoughts off his wife and attempted to focus again on the job before him. The mayor's wife would not be happy to find that her car wasn't ready in time. She had left explicit instructions for him to repair her car posthaste - with no "dilly-dallying".

"How's my favorite brother doing this morning?" Mike smiled at Nathan's words as his brother breezed into the office and settled down in one of the chairs across his desk. "How come you aren't elbow deep in grease right now?"

"I'm ordering a part." The lingering thoughts of his fight with Leanne left Mike's tone curt.

Nathan rested his elbows on the arms of the chair and steepled his fingertips over his lips. Mike looked quizzically at his younger brother, raising a tawny eyebrow.

"The cryptic and stony answer means you have a problem you can't fix."

"Just because you became the senior pastor, doesn't mean you can come in here and counsel me. I am still your older brother." Mike tried to lift his mouth in a grin but gave up. Leaning back in the chair, Mike admitted, "Me and Leanne had a fight last night. That's all."

At Nathan's chuckle, Mike asked, "And just what is so funny about the two of us fighting?"

"I'm sorry, but I'm trying to picture Leanne fighting." Nathan waved his hand and continued. "I mean, she can be a little stormy with her moods, but it is more like a pout than angry fighting mad."

Mike leaned back in the chair and shook his head. "I know. But it was like she was someone else last night."

"Leanne is probably stressed because of all that Karen is going through." Nathan asked, "When does she go to the doctor?"

"Karen goes to see Dr. Meston tomorrow." Mike sighed. "I just hope we are on speaking terms by the time we get to the appointment."

"That bad?" Nathan stared at his brother for a moment and then slapped the desk. "You know what you all need? You need to get away. Go up to that Triple-something Resort you all went to on your honeymoon."

Mike shook his head. "I thought so, too. Her parents offered to take the kids for a weekend. When I brought it up again last night, she blew up!" Mike ran a weary hand across his face. "I just don't know what to do about Karen *or* Leanne."

"I'll be praying for you. But don't forget to lean on God, too. From the slump in your shoulders, it looks like you are trying to carry this burden by yourself." Nathan stood to leave. "Read Psalm 68:19, big brother."

Mike chuckled and asked. "Are your trying to be like Dad? Point to a Scripture and then trail off in the wind."

"I'm perfecting the move. It's called the Scripture Bomb."

Mike put his hand over his eyes as if he could block out his brother's words.

Nathan continued his explanation. "You drop the Bible reference, and when the person picks up the Bible to read it for themselves, BOOM, it blows up in their heart, eradicating the lies, clearing the way for the truth."

"You need some serious help." Mike said between his laughter.

After a moment, the two sobered, and Nathan said, "So do you. Make sure you are going to God for guidance."

Mike watched his brother leave, but his words stayed with Mike all day. As he was underneath a car, his jumbled thoughts rattling around like the muffler he was fixing, he tried to sort out what had caused Leanne to become so vehemently opposed to leaving the kids with Deborah and Russell. He could tell her relationship with her mother was strained. The woman couldn't say a sweet word to Leanne if she ate syrup for a month straight. However, Leanne's anger about her parent's proposition seemed to stem from Russell, not her mom.

Mike shook his head. *But that just doesn't make any sense. She must have said "them", not "him" last night.* Though something still bothered him, Mike settled on that explanation because it was the only one that made sense.

Mike moved on to the car in bay two. The owner had brought it in yesterday for him to look at. Though there were no warning lights on, nor was there any clicking, clanking, or groaning coming from the engine, the owner had said he knew it just wasn't running right.

Mike understood where he was coming from. That was the description of his marriage. Though his marriage appeared to be fine, there was a serious problem underneath the hood. But unlike the car in bay two, he had no idea how to repair his marriage, because he couldn't pinpoint exactly what was wrong. On the surface, things looked fine. He had seen marriages fall apart because of adultery, finances, and constant bickering. But until last night, they barely disagreed. And the one thing they always disagreed on was Karen.

Mike's hands stilled and he dropped his tools down on a nearby table. Wiping a smudge of grease from his cheek, he stepped out from under the car and went back to the office to order the part he needed.

As he sat in his office, his hands stilled over the keyboard. Maybe he had been too quick to brush aside her concerns. He wanted to calm her fears, but maybe she just wanted to have him listen. Mike chuckled. *Not everything needs fixing.* Nathan said that to him all too often as the two were growing up.

Mike called home right after lunch and got the machine, so he left a message that he was leaving the shop a little early to check on his dad and then he'd be home for dinner. He was about to hang up, when he pulled the phone back to his ear. "I love you, Leanne. I don't want to fight anymore."

He hung up and was about to head back out to the bays, when he backtracked and returned to his desk. Picking up the office phone, he called her cell. When he didn't get an answer, he left another message for her to call as soon as possible. "Has something happened with Karen? Call me, honey, I'm worried."

After a few moments, he got a text message. "We're fine. Busy with the kids."

Mike sighed with relief, even though he could feel the coolness in her cryptic text.

He was about to head back out to the garage, but he sat down. Opening the Bible app on his phone, he scrolled to Psalm 68:19. "Praise be to the Lord, to God our Savior, who daily bears our burdens." He flipped through to compare the different translations, but the message was loud and clear. He had been trying to save their marriage, carry his burdens, as well as Leanne and Karen's. *Not everything needs fixing.* Maybe he also needed to remember that he is not the fixer.

"God, help me with my marriage." He sat at his desk for a moment, his heart so jumbled with emotions that his mouth couldn't form the words to pray what he needed to pray. So he sat, his eyes closed, but with his heart open. *Search me, search my heart and guide my path.* Mike felt like he needed to say more, but that was the only intelligible thing that seeped from his troubled spirit.

Later that afternoon, Mike's heart still felt troubled as he pulled into his parent's driveway.

"How are you feeling, Dad?"

"Not as good as I would if everyone stopped asking me how I feel," quipped his dad as he embraced Mike in a hearty hug.

"Well, I worry about you."

"Son, leave your worries with God."

"You aren't the first person to say that today." At

his dad's look, he explained. "It's nothing, just something Nathan said to me today."

"About Karen?" His mom asked, appearing from the kitchen and giving her son a hug.

The three settled down in the living room, and Mike watched his mom settle into the crook of his dad's arm. Sandra and Andrew McKinley had been married for 38 years, and they still cuddled, teased and flirted. Until this past week, Mike had thought he and Leanne were on the same path of his parents. He loved his wife more than he did when they first got married, and he was certain she felt the same. But the more he took a closer look at their marriage, the more he realized there were some cracks in his perfect relationship.

"We've been thinking, Son. We want to take the kids for the weekend. You and Leanne need to get away for a little while."

"Has Nathan been talking to you?"

The older couple exchanged curious looks, and then shook their heads.

At their denial, Mike hesitantly said, "I don't know that Leanne is up for it right now."

"Nonsense!" His mom cut him off. "I will talk to Leanne tomorrow when she comes to drop Rick off."

"Mom, I don't think that is such a good idea." All Mike could think about was the way Leanne had reacted last night. If she didn't want to leave Rick and Karen with her own parents, she wasn't going to leave them with his.

"Well, good idea or not, I am going to do it.

We've already reserved a room for you all this weekend."

Mike debated for a moment, and then shared some of his experience with Leanne's anger last night.

His mom was the first to speak. "I can't say I blame her. Her mom rarely has anything nice to say to her, and Leanne probably doesn't want to subject her own daughter to that treatment."

His mom shooed aside any further objections he had. "If she doesn't want to leave the kids with us, I'm sure she can tell me."

Recognizing he wasn't going to deter his mom, he simply asked, "Will you at least let me warn her first?"

"Sure," Sandra said with a backwards glance as she headed back to the kitchen to finish dinner.

After a moment, his dad said, "Mike, you have done wonders building Leanne up with your own words. Try washing her with a little of God's Word." At Mike's confused look, he added, "Read Ephesians five, verses twenty-five and twenty-six."

Mike grumbled. "Not another Scripture Bomb."

His dad laughed, and then slowly spread his hands in an exploding fashion. "BOOM."

"He told you about his idea?"

Andrew nodded. "I love it!" His dad laughed and added, "It may seem funny, but picking up the Bible and seeking out a Scripture is the physical representation of what your heart is doing: seeking God, and seeking his truth. If I just recite the verse to a person, they might hear it, but it is less active on their part."

Mike nodded in agreement. "I'll admit, I read the Scripture Bomb that Nathan dropped on me earlier."

"Did it explode in your heart?" Andrews asked with a wide grin.

Mike hung his head and nodded. "But I still feel troubled."

"The debris from the explosion is still settling. Keep reading and keep seeking Him."

"I will." Mike said and started to leave, but his dad stopped him.

"Son, don't settle for anything less than God's direction. When you *settle* your sights on Him alone, your spirit will be *settled*."

Mike nodded and headed toward the door, calling out to his dad over his shoulder. "You know, you two could have made a fortune writing ad campaigns."

"I'd rather write ads for God – I find myself far richer."

On the short drive home, Mike pondered what his dad had said. *Wash her with God's Word? Maybe he means pray Scripture over her.*

For the first part of their marriage, they always prayed together in the evening. But again, life seemed to wedge itself between them. They were busy with the kids, she was doing laundry, or one of them fell asleep. Little by little, their routine fizzled out.

He pulled up in the driveway and let out a little sigh of relief when he saw her car. A small part of him worried she wouldn't be home. He'd never seen her as angry as she was last night, and her continued silence throughout the day didn't ease his worries. He wasn't relishing telling her about his parents' gift, but he didn't want his mom to speak with her before he told her. The last thing their marriage needed was for her to think he'd gone behind her back. He valued the honesty their marriage always shared, and he didn't want a little lie of omission to make everything crumble now.

He walked in and froze in the doorway. She stood holding a glass dish and a tentative smile trembled on her lips. Accustomed to seeing her in sweats, he smiled at the pale pink dress that brought out the blue of her eyes.

"Hey, honey." He said, remembering to finally close the door.

She went to put the dish on the center of the table, and he jumped to move a vase out of the way. *Flowers? Had these always been here?*

After removing the oven mitts, she came to stand before him. Leaning up on her tip toes, she brushed a kiss across his cheeks. "Hey." It was the first word she had spoken to him since she had stormed out of their room last night, but the soft *hey* was sweeter than anything she could have said.

He threaded his fingers through her unbound hair at the nape of her neck, his eyes caressing the golden tresses that flowed over the back of his hand. His thumb rode along her jaw, tilting it upward for a lengthier kiss. "You look beautiful." He said after they parted.

It was then that he noticed the faint scratch along her cheek. "What happened?"

"Nothing," she said, trying to brush aside his concerns. "Karen got a little upset at the store today."

The store? With a crushed heart, he remembered his harsh words to her last night. Had he shamed her into going to the store today? "Leanne, about last night. I am so sorry for what I said, I..."

"No," she cut him off. "You were right. She has a hard time, but she can't stay in a box forever." Tears pooled in her eyes and she tried to avert her face, but Mike didn't let her.

"You were right, too. I haven't really been listening to you. All I've done was to try and ease your concerns, but I wasn't really listening to what you had to say. Maybe you just needed to talk." There was a hint of a question in his words, and she answered him with a nod. The tears fell down her cheeks, and she wrapped her arms around his neck. "Today has been awful."

"For me, too." He cradled the back of her head with one hand and wrapped his arm around her waist with the other. He held her there for a few moments while she cried.

"I love you so much." He pulled away from her a bit so he could look down at her.

"Me, too." She sniffled as she struggled to hold back the tears. "I was still so angry this morning, that while I was dusting, I knocked over our wedding picture." The tears came despite her efforts to squelch them, and he wiped the wetness gently from her cheeks.

"It's okay," he chuckled, "we can get a new frame."

She shook her head. "No, it was the glass. It was all cracked and shattered over our picture." A shudder tore through her as she tried to speak through the sobs that racked her body. "I just kept thinking, I don't want our marriage to be like that stupid glass."

He wrapped his arms around her again and pulled her close, letting her cry it out. He could feel the force of the sobs that wracked her body, and he tightened his arms around her in an effort to stave her tears.

*All because you were impatient, growing weary of always having to encourage her failing self-esteem.*

Rick chose that moment to come speeding down the hallway and into the room, wearing a yellow dump truck on his head like a helmet. He came to a halt in front of them. "Mommy's crying."

"Yes."

"Mommy cried at Whoop-Mart."

Rick's mispronunciation of Wal-Mart caused a strangled laugh to erupt from Leanne. Mike didn't miss the reference to the emotional day his wife had, and he was about to ask Leanne what happened, when she began giggling again. He looked down at his son again and realized that he was only wearing a shirt and his pull-ups, his sister's pink back pack strapped to his back, and of course, the dump truck as a helmet. Mike and Leanne dissolved into laughter while the two year old just looked at them as if *they* were the strange ones.

# Chapter Five

"Goodnight, Karen." Mike brushed a kiss on top of her head and then cracked the door on his way out.

Leanne met him in the hallway, and the two tiptoed back toward the kitchen. He hadn't brought up his parents' proposal at dinner, which had been filled with wonderful conversation, lots of laughter, and tender looks across the table.

Leanne turned to put the pans away which she had left drying in the rack. Mike came up behind her and took the pan from her as he turned her toward him. He kissed her forehead, stalling for a few more moments, loathe to ruin what had been a wonderful evening.

Draping her arms loosely around his neck, she asked, "Do you want to watch a movie together tonight?"

"Sure." He let his absentminded answer saunter out of his lips as he ran his hand down her unbound hair. "Have I ever told you how much I love it when you wear your hair down?"

She shook her head, and he smiled at the pretty blush that stained her cheeks at his compliment. "And this dress, is it new?"

She nodded this time. "I bought it today."

"At Whoop-Mart?"

She giggled. "Yes."

"It is a beautiful color; it brings out the color of your eyes."

"Aren't you full of compliments tonight?"

"Just appreciating the beauty that is before me."

He kissed her, letting his lips tell the rest of the emotions flooding his heart – regret, love, guilt, desire. The movie they had planned to watch, the conversation that they needed to have, all of it was a distant memory as she threaded her fingers through the hair on the nape of his neck.

He heard her moan, but it wasn't until she broke away from their kiss that he recognized her moan was one of frustration. When the phone rang again, she picked it up. "Hello?"

Mike swiped a hand down his face. Whoever it was, he hoped she would get rid of them quickly. He quietly put away the pans, half listening to his wife's side of the conversation.

"I'll have to check with Mike."

He turned toward her at the mention of his name.

His wife ignored his inquisitive look and continued her conversation. "I know, and I agree, she loves it there."

After a few moments, Mike's heart sunk as Leanne wrapped up her end of the conversation. "Thank you, Sandra."

*There goes our night.*

When Leanne hung up, he walked toward her, taking her gently by the shoulders. "I wanted to warn you before she talked to you." He smiled sheepishly. Hoping to recapture a little of the evening, he pulled her close. "I got a little distracted."

Leanne smiled at his words, but the flirtatious

spark had fizzled a little with the conversation. He could see the concern in her eyes.

"Look, if you don't think she's ready for this, we won't go."

Leanne fiddled with a button on his shirt, not looking in his eyes as she said, "I'm worried."

Mike heard the silent "but" dangling from her words and his hope dangled there with it. After a few moments, she hesitantly answered. "But I know we need this time alone."

Thinking about her trip to the store, Mike didn't want her to feel pressured because of his angry words last night. "Leanne, I know you were opposed to leaving Karen with your parents..."

"It's different!" She cut him off, and he heard the restrained anger in her words.

Gently cupping her face, he forced her to look at him. "I don't want you to feel like you have to because of what I said last night."

She pulled his hands down and stepped away from his hold. "I said it's different." Walking toward the living room, she threw over her shoulder. "How about that movie?"

He heard the forced jovialness in her tone, but decided to let the discussion drop for now.

Built-in bookshelves that he had made with his dad flanked either side of the fireplace. She was looking through their DVDs when he walked into the room.

"What do you want to watch?" She asked as he came up behind her.

Placing a hand on the fireplace mantle, he bent down and brushed a kiss along her neck. "You choose. Do you want popcorn?"

She pulled out a DVD and handed it to him. "Sure."

When she started to head for the kitchen again, he put a restraining hand on her waist and steered her over to the couch. "No, you sit down and let me make it." With one hand on the back of the couch, he leaned down, his lips hovering over hers. "Thank you for a beautiful dinner."

After a quick kiss, he put the DVD in and then jogged into the kitchen. While the popcorn bag inflated in the microwave, he placed one hand on the counter, tapping lightly as he worried over her agreement to take the trip. As he fiddled with what he should do about it, the verse he read to today trickled across his mind. "He daily bears our burdens."

*God, guide me in our marriage and as a father.* Mike silently prayed. After a few moments, he added, *I don't know what my dad meant by wash her with Your words, but help me to understand.*

The microwave chimed its completion, but the acrid smell of burnt popcorn filled the air. As he dumped the contents of the bag into the bowl, the black center portion confirmed that he had overcooked it. *Great*, he thought. He threw the contents in the trashcan and popped another bag. When he finally returned to the living room with the bowl of popcorn and two bottles of water, the movie had already started. Setting it down on the table, he began, "Sorry it took so long, but I burned..."

He stopped mid-sentence as he gazed down at his wife sleeping peacefully, her head propped on one arm. With a sigh, Mike gathered his wife in his arms. As he carried her to their room, she stirred briefly, just enough to lay her head on his shoulder and throw her arm around his neck.

Kicking their door open with his foot, he walked to the bed and tenderly placed her on the bed. Careful not to wake her, he gently slipped her shoes off and slid her legs under the covers. Sitting next to her, Mike brushed her hair back from her face, which was so soft and peaceful in sleep.

Mike remembered the first time he saw her. Despite the fact that he was three years older than her, they had both attended college orientation at the same time. Mike knew he wanted to run his father's garage. After graduation, he worked in the garage for three years, hoping to take over the business. But his father insisted he get a degree before assuming the reigns of leadership.

When he walked into the administration building that day, she was standing in line at the registrar's office. Her hair was longer then and reached almost to her waist. The sides of her hair were pulled up, but there was one long strand near her forehead that had escaped its bonds. When she turned her head his way, their eyes met. He had never seen a lighter pair of blue eyes - ice blue like a Siamese cat. But there was nothing cold about the tentative smile that took hold of her face when he winked at her. She shyly tucked the strand of hair behind her ear, but didn't break their gaze until her stepfather put his hand on the small of her back and whispered something in her ear.

The smile faded and she turned back in line, but her sweet smile had carried him back home in euphoria. He couldn't wait for the chance to meet her again.

On a few occasions, their class schedules would intertwine. He tried to get her attention after class, but she always rushed out before he had a chance.

It wasn't until their junior year when her car broke down that he had a chance to speak with her. He had taken it upon himself to fix her car personally, even taking the time to wash and detail it. When he drove the car to her house, he had placed a small vase with three roses in the cup holder in the center console.

Driving up to her parents' house, she came rushing out before he could even ring the doorbell.

She stood before him, the afternoon sun glistening off her golden hair and a tentative smile on her lips. "Thank you, but, like I said on the phone, you didn't have to drive it here. I could have picked it up." She tucked the strand hair behind her ear, and then reached to take the keys from his extended hand. "How much do I owe you?"

"Nothing." He closed his hand before she could grab the keys. "Just a date."

It was then that she finally looked at him. "A

date?"

"Yes," he smiled and sucked in his breath at the impact her eyes had on his stomach. She was the most beautiful girl her had ever seen. "Dinner? Even lunch at the student union?" When she still didn't respond, he added with a hopeful grin. "Coffee in between classes?"

"Um," she looked over her shoulder as her stepfather came out, "I don't know."

"Just one date." At her hesitation, he added, "Think about it." He handed her the keys.

He shook her stepfather's hand as the man came to stand next to Leanne. Placing an arm around her shoulder, Russell said, "So you're the young man who came to our little Lee-Lee's aid the other day?"

Mike saw Leanne's cheeks flush a pretty pink. Though he found the blush quite fetching, he didn't want to embarrass her or make her feel uncomfortable. "I was happy to help."

When the man took out his wallet, Mike halted him. "No charge."

"Nonsense," Russell began, but Mike cut him off.

"Really, the work and parts were minimal. Like I said, I was happy to help."

With a brief goodbye, Mike left, but, as he drove by, he didn't miss the small smile on her lips as she spotted the vase in the car.

It had taken her several months to actually agree to go on a real date with him. At first, she would only meet him for lunch, or as he suggested, for a few borrowed moments between classes. After a month of settling for stolen seconds with her on campus, Mike was able to convince her to go out to dinner with him, but she would only meet him at the location of their dates – she never allowed him to pick her up.

Mike hated her reluctance to open up to him, but he attributed it to her shy nature. One night he finally took a chance and asked her. "Why don't you let me come and pick you up this time?"

She shrugged and looked away, a pout on her pretty lips. "What's the big deal either way? We are together."

"Because this feels like we are two friends hanging out together." He pulled her close and whispered. "You are special to me, and I want to treat you the way you deserve to be treated."

Her eyes misted at his words and her pout softened into a smile. It was then that he realized every kind word he spoke to her was one more thread he removed as he unwound her from the shyness and self-doubt that bound her.

Now, as he looked down on his sleeping wife, he whispered, "I'm sorry."

His perfunctory kisses, and flat, meaningless, *Things will be fine*, were binding her more than unwinding her. Mike wondered if that is what his father was alluding to when he said wash Leanne with words.

Mike paused. *No, what did Dad say? Wash her with God's Word.*

As Mike rose and went to turn off the lights and lock up the house, he thought about what his dad meant.

Moments later, when he slid into bed, he wrapped his arms around his wife. He buried his lips in her hair, breathing in the floral scent of her shampoo. Closing his eyes, he began to whisper a prayer. The prayer was born out of love, grew into hope and matured into understanding that God would, and always was, working in their marriage.

"I love this woman, God. Please help me set her free from the pain her mother has inflicted on her. Those harsh words can be healed by Your love." He kissed her shoulder lightly, so as not to wake her. "But I'd be honored, Lord, if you would use me."

Mike fell asleep with the prayer still trotting through his mind.

---

Leanne let her tears fall unheeded on the pillow. Mike's prayer was sweet, kind, and full of the love he felt for her. He kept talking about washing her with words, and the picture sent more tears to her eyes as guilt and shame pierced her conscience. She wanted to be washed. She *needed* to be washed. Her past had been a silent thief throughout the years, lurking in the shadows, threating to steal everything from her.

Now all these cracks were appearing in her life and those secrets were threatening to escape. Mike had no idea how much his love had cleansed her over the years, and his guilt-laced prayer made her want to roll over in his arms and hush him. She wanted to hold him, comfort him, and, most all, tell him the truth.

But the truth would hurt him more than what he was going through now.

Instead, she listened to his prayer with a thirsty heart that drank every word of love in, and a guilt-laden mind that cried foul.

# Chapter Six

"Welcome to the Triple R Ranch and Resort!" The young lady behind the counter beamed as she began the process of checking them in. "I see you are in one of our Restoration Suites. Did you leave your cell phones at home, or will you need to place them in our safe?"

Mike and Leanne looked at each other in confusion. "What do you mean?"

"Our Restoration suites are media free rooms. There is no TV or internet access in the rooms. We ask that you either leave your cell phone at home, or, if you feel more comfortable, you can leave it in the hotel safe."

"We have to give them to you?" Leanne asked warily, wondering how the McKinley's would contact them if something happened with Karen.

The woman behind the counter shook her head. "No, but we ask that if you choose to keep your phones with you, the ringer is turned off and that you do not use it in the common areas."

Mike shrugged and handed his phone to the woman. Leanne pulled her phone out of her purse but held it close to her chest. "What if your parents call?"

"We can call them when we get to the room and let them know how to reach us."

After a few moments of hesitation, Leanne relinquished her phone.

Their room was similar to the suite they had been

in for their honeymoon. A large king-sized bed sat in the middle of the room, covered with a pale yellow bedspread with small maroon paisleys. Under the window sat a sofa the same pale yellow as the bedspread, with maroon throw pillows.

Kneeling on the sofa, Leanne looked out the window into the courtyard below. She saw a larger version of the fountain that was in the lobby; it was surrounded by several semi-circular stone benches.

"They must have retreats up here or something."

Mike knelt behind her, placing his chin on her shoulder, wrapping his arms around her waist. She leaned back into his body, relishing in the feel of his closeness, his warmth and strength.

"It's beautiful." He kissed her neck. "Just like you."

She turned sideways in his embrace and tried to relax. But she couldn't free her mind from her worries about Karen. "We should call your parents first."

His words were punctuated with short pecks on her lips. "Okay, I will - if you promise to stop worrying."

"I'm sorry." She placed a hand on his chest. "I just have this feeling that something is wrong."

Mike sighed and walked toward the phone on the nightstand. Leanne didn't miss the weariness on his face, and she silently vowed she would make it up to him.

"Hey, Mom, just wanted to let you know they confiscated our phones."

Leanne heard him laugh before he added, "You mean you *conveniently* forgot to tell us."

Mike winked at Leanne, and she smiled lightly. She was worried about Karen, Mike's prayers still haunted her, her secrets were rising up like bile in her throat, and now she could tell Mike was disappointed in her.

*Please don't let me lose him!*

"I know Leanne would not forgive me if I didn't ask how the kids are doing."

Leanne shot him a grateful look and sat down next to him on the bed. He tilted the receiver so she could hear his mom speak as well.

"Tell her the kids are doing fine. Karen is snuggled on the couch reading with Grandpa, and Rick and I are about to go play outside."

"Thanks, Mom." Mike said, and before he could hang up, Leanne added, "Call us if there's any trouble!"

She didn't miss the look that passed over Mike's face at her hurried comment.

Looking chagrined, she mumbled, "I'm sorry."

He laid back on the bed, and she scooted closer to him. With her hip near his hip, she reached her hand across his body, resting it on the bed near his waist. Gratitude for his patience and love washed over her, and the emotion overwhelmed her. She tried to turn her head before he saw her tears, brushing them away with her free hand - but it was too late.

"Hey, why the tears?"

Leanne sniffled. "I am not worthy of your love,

but I am so thankful for it. Please know that."

Without another word, he pulled her down next to him. With her head resting on his chest, the two lay on the bed, lost in their own thoughts. She listened to the steady rhythm of his heartbeat as he gently stroked her unbound hair.

"I do love you, Leanne."

She felt the rumble of his words emanate from his chest. The words should have sent a thrill through her heart, but it was the preceding pause that caused her concern.

*Why did he pause? Is he unsure of his feelings?*

Leanne turned her head so she could look at him. Resting her chin on her interlaced hands that lay on his muscular chest, she watched an array of emotions play across his perfect, chiseled features.

She drew a fortifying breath and leaned up over him to kiss him. Her blonde hair created a curtain around their faces, and he gently brushed it back. His hands and his words gently stalled her lips' descent. "I've noticed you've been wearing your hair down lately."

"You said you liked it when I wore it down, so..." Maybe it was the way that he was staring at her, or maybe it was just being back here, but she felt just as nervous as she had on their wedding night. She kicked aside the reminder that she had been nervous for a different reason on their honeymoon.

*How different is it?* Her conscience protested. *You are still harboring lies and trying to earn a love you are not worthy of.*

She brushed off her nagging thoughts and ran a line of kisses across his cheek until her lips met his.

Again, he stalled her kiss from deepening. "But I love you no matter how you wear your hair, or how you dress. I'll love you no matter what."

He held her face cradled in his palms. The feel of his rough skin on her soft cheeks was no different than the feel of his words as they slid down her heart – a little abrasive, but it still felt so deliciously sweet.

She had vowed after his prayer the other night to never let him know the truth and never to let him down again. But his one statement, and the look of unconditional love shining in his steel gray eyes, made her want to let go of her secret.

Mike, her sweet, handsome, and all too perfect husband, would never understand her dark, bitter, ugly and soiled past. What was that Scripture that Andrew McKinley was always saying, something about the truth setting you free?

*Ha!* Leanne thought bitterly. *The only freedom I will get from revealing the truth is Mike will make himself free of me.*

With a strength and determination born from years of treacherous self-preservation, she wrestled that idealistic notion down. That same determination fed her desire to please him, and she kissed away his initial hesitation.

He rolled her underneath him, pulling his head back to hinder her seduction. She saw confusion and some unnamed emotion skitter across his features as he brushed a tear that rolled down her temple.

*Mike, I can do this! This is the one thing I know how to do. Please don't stop me.*

Her silent plea stayed locked in her thoughts, but her lips did not stay still, as she pulled his head down for a kiss that incinerated all his hesitation.

When he first whispered her name it was a cry for her to stop, but her lips seized the rest of his demand, sapping his desire to impede her actions. Her name tore from his lips again, this time a tangled mess of confusion and trepidation. Finally, he cried her name out in defeat as he surrendered to her hands, her lips, and her body, as she silently vowed to make him happy, to make him see her as worthy, even though she knew the truth to be otherwise.

---

The soft sound of Mike's snores filled her ears, and she wished she could sleep as soundly as he did.

Carefully, so as not to wake him from his nap, she extracted herself from his embrace and got dressed. Leaving him a quick note, she silently closed the door behind her.

She rode the elevator down to the main floor. Leanne figured she could walk around for a little bit to kill time before lunch.

As she wandered around the grounds of the resort, she got lost in thoughts of their past.

When they first got married, Mike's love had healed her, strengthened her, and she had leaned heavily on him. Maybe she had leaved too heavily on him, she thought. Maybe that is where his weariness had come into play lately.

But his love was like a drug, and she needed it. The more she had it, the harder she tried to hold it.

She had remembered when they were dating, she had almost lost him for that same reason. The morning had started out with her mother's usual criticisms, and her stepfather had been questioning everything about her relationship with Mike.

"I just don't think she should be so involved with this boy, Deborah." Russell had argued during breakfast. "I mean, she's got another semester left of her studies..."

"She is lucky to have found someone, and surprisingly, her grades haven't slipped all that much."

Leanne hated when they talked about her as if she wasn't there. She found the courage to speak up. "I am not going to stop seeing him."

"Young lady!" Though it was her mother who protested, Leanne's eyes were burrowing into her stepfather, silently defying him. "Your father is paying your way through college; it would do you well to remember to respect him."

*Stepfather*! Her thoughts screamed, but she mumbled an obedient, "Yes, ma'am."

Russell reached across the table and laid his hand on top of hers. "Lee-Lee, I just want what is best for you."

Pulling her hand out from beneath his, she jumped up. "I have to get to class or I'm going to be late."

She stormed off before they could say anything

else. But when she ran into Mike later, she had kissed him with a passion and a freedom she had never done before. When they kissed, she felt whole. When he smiled down at her, brushed her hair back, and said his incredibly sweet things to her, she felt healed. And when they parted, she felt empty.

Later that night, as he was dropping her off after their date, she kissed him in that same manner. She could see he was struggling with his passion for her, but she didn't want to stop.

"I think we need to stop, Leanne." Mike said between labored breaths.

She wanted to ask why, but instead she leaned across the center console in his truck to pull his head in for another kiss.

Mike pulled back, and her brow furrowed with confusion. He brushed back a strand of her hair, and his gentle touch caused her to close her eyes, as if she could hold onto the sweetness she felt in his touch.

But Mike's next words chased that sweetness away. "Leanne, I've never…I mean, I want to wait until we are married." Tilting his head to the side, he asked, "Don't you?"

"Of course," she lied.

She looked away under the guise of straightening her shirt. Tears filled her eyes, first with the pain of his rejection, and then a twinge of guilt that swiftly followed.

After a moment, it dawned on her what he said. "You want to marry me?"

"Well, of course. Why else would I be dating

you?"

She had to avert her gaze from his steel gray eyes. They were so different. He was so good, sweet and kind. *Unspoiled and perfect Mike saddled with me for life,* she had thought with an inward snort of derision. *How could I ever measure up to what he thinks I am.*

Leanne pulled herself out of her memories. *I will try, Mike. I promise I will try to be everything you wanted me to be.*

The wandering course of her thoughts had led her no closer to a real resolution for the guilt and doubt that plagued her. On the other hand, her physical wandering had brought her to the courtyard, where she found herself in front of the fountain she and Mike had looked down on from their room.

Sitting on one of the stone benches, Leanne looked at the monstrous fountain before her. She remembered seeing a similar statue in the lobby when they were here for their honeymoon, but this one was different. It had two sides, one with a crumbling wall and water seeping through the cracks. The inside of the left half of the fountain had a couple with their hands over the cracks, trying to stop the flow of water seeping through. The other half of the fountain had a no cracks in the walls. The water was directed around the wall, and the embracing bronze couple in the middle remained dry.

The plaque in front of the fountain read:

**"*Anyone who listens to my teaching and follows***

*it is wise, like a person who builds a house on solid rock. Though the rain comes in torrents and the floodwaters rise and the winds beat against that house, it won't collapse because it is built on bedrock. But anyone who hears my teaching and doesn't obey it is foolish, like a person who builds a house on sand. When the rains and floods come and the winds beat against that house, it will collapse with a mighty crash."*
*Matthew 7:24-27*

*A solid foundation is essential to any building. From temperature and moisture fluctuations, the weight it must bear, and the natural settling that occurs, a foundation is under constant stress. If the foundation is not properly built, this stress will cause cracks to appear. If left untreated, these cracks can grow and lead to more damage.*

Aside from the reference to foundations, Leanne didn't understand how the Scripture and the information in the plaque went together. But the couple desperately trying to plug the cracks wrested a scoffing laugh from her. *That's how I feel, like I am trying to stop the flood from pouring into our marriage.*

Conviction pierced her heart. One of those floods was her past, which seemed to be battering their marriage more and more these days. She tried to reason through her guilt at the lies she had told to save Mike from the awful truth of her past.

She reasoned - *I wasn't really lying; I just withheld things. I'm sure he has secrets that he hasn't told me.*

Then she rationalized - *If I were to tell him the truth, it would hurt him.*

Finally, she persuaded her nagging conscience to keep silent. *If he knew, he would probably leave, and that would hurt our children.*

But no matter how she tried to convince herself she was justified in her actions, the feeling in the pit of her stomach wouldn't go away.

She wondered what Mike would do if he were in her shoes.

Leanne had not started going to church until they were dating, and she only began attending as an excuse to get out of her house and spend more time with Mike. She kicked at a loose pebble on the ground.

*Another lie by omission.*

When he first invited her to church, she was happy for a reason to spend some time away from home and with him. She had never disabused him of his notion that she was a Christian, and, over the years, she began to consider herself one. But lately, the sermons and Bible studies were convicting her that there was more to being a Christian than what she was doing now. She didn't know what it was, and to ask would mean revealing the truth.

Leanne looked at the left side of the statue again.

That was definitely her, desperately trying to plug up all the holes her lies had caused, but the water was rising, and she felt as if she was going to drown at any moment.

A worker came and sat next to her on the bench, pulling Leanne from her morose thoughts.

The woman opened a brown paper bag, pulling out a small note. The woman smiled as she read it, and then pulled out her sandwich, turning to Leanne. "I love this statue. I usually try to have my lunch here."

Leanne smiled at her; her nametag said Tracy.

"Are you here for the readying, restoring or rejuvenating?"

Leanne shrugged. "When they checked my husband and I in, the woman said we were in the restoration suite."

"Have you signed up for the classes?"

Leanne shook her head.

The woman turned toward her, eagerness dripping from her smile. "You two can't leave without attending at least one class."

Leanne didn't want to spend her one weekend away sitting in a class hearing some lecture. But the woman gushed on. "If you are here to restore anything in your marriage, or your walk with Christ, I'd suggest the Firm Foundation class."

"The statue also has a class?"

The young woman giggled. "They teach you how to build your life centered around the truth of God's Word." Tracy gestured to her with the tip of her triangular cut sandwich. "This afternoon, they have a special one for couples - for marriage. You and your husband should go."

Standing to leave, Leanne smiled. "Well, I will have to tell my husband about it."

Leanne walked away, glancing back briefly at the young woman and the statue. The foundation for their marriage was built on love. They weren't a troubled marriage, plagued by adultery or anything like that. They just had a lot of storms. Like the couple, they were just busy trying to plug up the cracks. But their foundation was solid because they loved each other, and no class was going to erase their storms. It wasn't going to change the fact that she had a daughter that was falling apart, or a husband who was inching away. What she needed was some time spent in her husband's arms, which is where she always found strength. A weekend in his arms was all she needed to be restored, and when she returned to Hamilton, she would be fine.

# Chapter Seven

Mike woke slowly, reaching for Leanne but found the spot next to him empty and cold.

He sat up, looking around the room for her. Swinging his legs over the side of the bed, he donned his pants and padded over to the restroom. Not finding her there either, he walked over to the coffee table, where he saw the note she left him.

*Gone for a walk, sweet dreams, my love.*

He caught a glimpse of her out the window, sitting in the courtyard before the fountain. Seeing the sadness on her face, his own shoulders slumped. He had enjoyed her passion in bed, but...

Mike swiped his hand down his face in frustration, unable to put his finger on what was troubling him. He kissed and hugged Leanne often, because it was like she needed the physical acts of love to reassure her, just as she needed his verbal confirmation to build her up. But no matter how many times he hugged her, kissed her or told her how loved she was, it was never enough.

He felt like a heel. He knew how much her mother hurt her with her words, and he had spent their marriage trying to build her up with his loving words. But after all these years, it was like she still needed his constant reassurance. His shoulders sank with the weight of his job, and the guilt of his weariness.

*Don't look for holes,* he warned. After all, hadn't

his father told him to wash her with words? Mike found a Bible on the coffee table and looked up the verse his dad had mentioned. His fingers flew across the pages as he searched for the book of Ephesians. "Chapter five, verses twenty-five and twenty-six," Mike said, and continued to read the verses out loud in the empty room. "For husbands, this means love your wives, just as Christ loved the church. He gave up his life for her to make her holy and clean, washed by the cleansing of God's word."

Sitting down on the couch, Mike rested his head in his hands. "God, I do love her. I would give my life to cleanse her of the hurt her mom has caused her."

His prayer died on his lips, as if it was holding its breath for the revelation that teetered on the edge of his mind. He still didn't understand what his father meant by wash her with God's Word. He raked his hand down his face in frustration. He whispered the last part of the verse, hoping understanding would dawn on him. But when none came, he finished his prayer. "Lord, help my words encourage and build her up, help my words to pierce through that pain."

He turned at the sound of the card key sliding through the door.

Leanne stood just inside the doorway, looking around in confusion. "Was someone on the phone? I thought I heard you talking?" She asked as she closed the door.

"I was just praying." He gathered her in his arms, resting his cheek against her hair, his prayer still echoing in his heart as he asked, "Did you have a good walk?"

"I met a worker at the fountain. She said they have classes here."

Her shrug let him know she didn't really care for the idea, but something within his spirit made him ask. "What kind of classes?"

"She was talking about a Firm Foundation class for marriages. I guess they have it at that weird statue." She pulled her head back and looked up at him. "Did you have a nice nap?"

"Yes." He held her for a few moments, running a hand lightly over her hair. "I think we should attend that class. I'm sure that's why my parents gave us this trip."

Leanne shrugged. "If you want; I guess so." He could tell by the look on her face that it was the last thing she wanted to do, but Leanne was always quick to please him.

Easy going, peacemaker, humble and soft spoken…the words he often used to describe his wife tumbled through his mind along with guilt and…Mike struggled to pinpoint that unnamed emotion that dogged him - *frustration*? Mike quickly untangled the thought from winding through his mind, but the thought persisted.

After a quick lunch, the couple made their way to the fountain. Mike read the plaque and looked down at Leanne. "That is pretty amazing, and what a great message." He felt guilty for his earlier thoughts. After all of the stressors they had been through lately, he was sitting there grumbling about his wife needing to lean on him.

Taking his wife's hands in his own, he admitted. "I am not sure I've done such a great job of making sure He was the foundation in our marriage."

He saw her brow furrow as she looked at the statue, finally returning her gaze to his. "He who?"

"Jesus."

She looked at the statue again, and her lips formed a silent "oh."

Her words trailed off, and Mike began to slowly understand what his dad and God had been speaking to him. Not only did their marriage not have a foundation in Christ, but he was beginning to wonder how firm her foundation in Christ was too. She couldn't accept his love as enough, because she hadn't learned to accept the fact that God's love was enough to carry her through everything in this life and beyond. Everything she was operating under was falsehoods -truth twisted by a bitter mom and her own failing self-confidence.

Cupping her face between his palms, he gently rested his forehead against hers. Mike closed his eyes and breathed deep, exhaling the words, "I'm sorry."

"For what?"

"For not doing what God called me to do."

She was still gazing up at him in confusion when the resort employee came and asked that everyone take their seats. With his arm around her waist, he looked over her shoulder as they read the Bible passages together. How many Sundays had they sat like this at church, his arm laying across the back of the pew, Leanne tucked into the crook of his arm? He could smell the floral scent of her perfume, and he could feel the soft brush of her hair against his arm as she turned to look up at him. She was more beautiful than the day he had met her. Never had he loved her more. Yet he had blindly let her sit in ignorance.

Mike struggled to focus on the class.

"Like the plaque states, marriages come with ups and downs. Whatever you choose to have as the foundation in your marriage, it must be able to bear the hot and the cold times. It must also be able to handle all the shifting circumstances in your life. Your relationship status didn't stop changing once you got married. Marriages move from newlywed status, to new parents, to empty nesters, to retirement. And circumstances can create further changes - illness, job loss, infertility...the list goes on."

Mike looked behind the man to the fountain, and easily recognized that they were the couple desperately trying to plug the holes.

"I personally think this is one of the best points on the list, and every time I teach this class, I stress it - especially to newlyweds. The plaque says a foundation must be able to bear the weight of everything within the structure. From the furniture to the occupants, the foundation must carry that load."

The man pointed to the cracks in the wall. "The majority of the cracks in marriages come from having a foundation that is not able to carry the weight."

The man circled the group, and there was a heavy

silence in the air. He stopped before Mike and Leanne. "How long have you all been married?"

"Seven years."

"Do you have any children?"

"Two."

"So the foundation of your house must hold the weight of four people. Two of which are growing at a rapid rate, no doubt."

His comment sent a murmur of laughter through the crowd. "But each of those individuals also carries with them a bag...an invisible bag. Worries, issues, their past."

He turned to Mike again and he asked, without knowing the magnitude of his question. "How much do those bags weigh?"

Mike looked at Leanne, and before he could answer, she spoke up. "Sometimes you think you know, but you really can't understand how heavy the other person's bag is."

"That's right, and some of us carry around pretty heavy bags." Though the man moved on, Mike and Leanne stayed locked in their gaze, only interrupted by the squeaky wheels of a cart being rolled into the courtyard by another resort employee.

"If everyone will come up and grab a backpack."

As Mike and Leanne approached the cart, the woman who handed them their backpacks smiled at Leanne. "I'm glad you decided to come to the class. It's great, huh?"

The bag was not that heavy, at first, but as they made their rounds, it began to dig into his shoulders.

He looked down at Leanne, who was visibly struggling with the weight of her bag. He stopped to help her adjust the pack a little, and the man caught sight of them. He thought they were going to be singled out. "Why don't you take the load off her shoulders and carry it around for her?"

Once Mike had Leanne's backpack on his shoulders, the man asked Leanne. "Feel better?"

She nodded and they made another lap around the circle, with Mike adjusting his cumbersome load twice on the way. Again, the man stopped them. "You said you had kids, right?"

Mike answered, "Yes, two..."

The man handed him two more backpacks, but stopped and asked, "You don't have any back problems, do you?"

Mike answered with a good-natured laugh. "I might after this exercise."

The man helped Mike put on the other bags, and Mike immediately felt the difference in the weight on his shoulders and back. Leanne looked concerned, and the man picked up on this. "You feel bad he's shouldering all of this himself while you are running around free, right?" Taking one of the bags off Mike's shoulders, he put it back on Leanne's. "Now you feel like you are doing your part, right?"

Mike was happy when the man finally called an end to the illustration, and he gladly surrendered his heavy load. The man thanked them for their participation and then continued. "Our shoulders were never meant to carry those bags. Your spouse's shoulders weren't meant to carry those bags. Your marriage cannot survive under the weight of shifting circumstances, your burdens, and the temperature fluctuations in your love for one another if the foundation for your marriage is *only* your love for each other."

Leanne looked perplexed, and Mike was worried that the man would leave them with that spiritual nugget of wisdom and close out the class, but thankfully, the man continued. "Christ is the only foundation for your marriage that will be able to withstand all of it, and more."

Mike prayed that Leanne would understand the man's words as he continued. "It begins with a personal relationship. Each individual in the marriage must have a firm foundation of Christ in their own life. Then, as a team, you must choose to be guided by, and live your life by, His truth. Empower and build each other up, brick by brick, with His word. Then you will have built a marriage that can weather storms, because the foundation is firmly and correctly built."

The class ended with prayer, and as Mike and Leanne bowed their heads together, Mike vowed to help build her up with God's Word, and help unearth any lies that had settled into her heart and disguised themselves as truth.

After the prayer ended, the couples milled about, some talking with the teacher, some with each other. A man came over and good-naturedly teased him about the backpacks. While he laughed with the man,

Mike sensed Leanne's quiet contemplation.

*God, help me help her understand.* Mike silently prayed.

Mike and Leanne eventually made their way through the crowd and headed toward their room. He could tell the class had an impact on her. Once inside, he sat down on the sofa and patted the seat next to him. She curled up into his arms, and he kissed the top of her head. "So what did you think about the class?"

She didn't answer right away, and at first, he thought she might have fallen asleep. Finally, she answered. "I never really thought about what he said before." After another pause, she added, "but it makes sense."

She turned her head to look at him, rubbing his shoulders. "Are your shoulders okay?"

Mike chuckled, "Yes, they're fine." He kissed her forehead, and added, "Nathan told me to look up Psalm 68:19, which pretty much talks about the same thing." He sat up, and opened the Bible to the passage and read it to her. "It's a simple little verse, but powerful."

She nodded, still contemplative.

"What are you thinking about?" He asked.

She looked at him, and there were tears hovering on the ends of her lashes. He wanted to reach for her, to brush back those tears before they had a chance to wet her cheeks. But something within him stilled his movements, as if her salvation would come in the spilling of those tears. As if she couldn't be healed until her tears had run their course. She looked at him, and sadness wound its way through his heart.

As much as he wanted to comfort her, his spirit held him back. But from the look on her face, it appeared as if her spirit was urging her forward, but her heart, twisted with lies and hurt, held her back. Her lips trembled, visible proof of her struggle. "I don't know."

He stayed where he was, physically and mentally, silent in the wake of her uncertain beginnings. As if his words would be a distraction, he silently prayed for her.

"I guess I am just wondering how..." uncertainty softened her words and gave her pause. "I just don't know how strong of a Christian I really am."

He let out a breath that he hadn't realized he was holding. "Leanne, I think..." His words trickled into nothingness. Mike had been about to utter some platitude, meant to encourage her, but he realized these were just his words. A memory of a similar conversation when they were dating came to his mind. She had said something about not being a good Christian, and he had thrown out some words to encourage her. He thought it was her wavering self-esteem buckling under another tirade from her mother. But had they been born of a searching heart? A searching heart he had left wandering around blindly for years.

*It'll be fine.* His monotonous platitude came back to haunt him. Again, he really hadn't been listening. The fixer in him had wanted to restore her downcast face, but all he did was stick a Band-Aid on her hurt.

"I think we both need to start looking closely at God's truth." He finally said, brushing a strand from her forehead. "I think we've both been operating under some faulty notions, and I say we start fixing our foundations."

The tears gave up their grip on her lashes and plopped down on her cheeks. Mike's spirit gave reign to his heart's desire, and he kissed the tears off her cheeks. The couple settled back on the couch, snuggled in each other's arms and the Bible open on their laps. Through the late hours of the night, they flipped through pages, read and discussed the verses, and rededicated their marriage and their lives to Christ. And as the darkness loosened its grip on the night, so a new light dawned in their marriage.

# Chapter Eight

Wrapping the towel around her body, Leanne wiped the steam from the bathroom mirror before running a comb through her hair. Though they had originally planned to visit the shops in town and look for a wedding gift for Nathan and Kristina, their late night Bible study had led to a quick room-service breakfast followed by a long nap. Mike was still sleeping when she woke up, so she decided to shower before the two of them headed out to the town for lunch.

Leanne had felt good last night as she let go of the fear that had been holding back her questions over the years. She had always feared that Mike would look down on her, or think less of her, if she admitted her fledgling faith. But in his true form, Mike had walked through each verse with her last night, and even confessed some of his struggles in his own faith. The only dark spot on last night was her nagging conscience that was crying foul at her deceptions. Her normal justifications weren't doing anything to calm the stormy, turbulent feeling that was churning in her stomach. The more excuses she came up with, the more unsettled she felt. The more she tried to silence the voice that said *tell the truth*, the louder it got.

However, in the end, one fearful thought was louder than all others. While she wanted to trust in this firm foundation concept, and God's ability to withstand all the storms, she wasn't comfortable yet with putting it to the test. There were always consequences for your bad decisions, and Leanne McKinley was a woman riddled with wrong decisions.

The unsettled feeling remained, so, in an effort to stave off the nagging voice within her, she vowed to tell Mike the truth when the time was right...sometime soon. She wanted to enjoy this new start to their marriage. She wanted to coast along in peaceful waters before she rocked the boat.

She slipped into her clothes after blow drying her hair, and walked out into the room to find a suitcase open on the bed and Mike throwing their clothes into it.

"What happened?" Leanne asked, panic rising in her voice at the look on his face.

"Dad collapsed and he was rushed to the hospital. I guess Karen was there when it happened and she had a big meltdown. She bit her arm hard enough to break the skin." Though he didn't stop his packing process, she heard the catch in his voice as he tried to suppress his emotion.

Without a word, Leanne turned to help him, and they were packed and rolling their suitcases to the car within a few minutes. She checked them out while he loaded the car. The two were descending the winding roads of the mountain in no time. No words were spoken as the car looped its way along the highway, and the only evidence that the two were aware of the other's presence was when he reached out his hand for hers. The action was not new, but the motive behind it was.

Mike always reached for her hand to give her strength, to let her know he was there for her, and to confirm his love. This time, he needed her strength, he needed her reassurance, and he needed her love to encourage him. *I just took my first steps yesterday, and now You are asking me to take off in a run? How in the world am I going to help him, God?*

All her failures overcame her at once, and she struggled under the weight of them. She fought to surface, to draw a single breath as they pulled her down into the swirling pool of self-pity. Until her heart whispered, *I need you to help me carry this God. For me and for Mike.*

They stayed like that for the remainder of the ride, hands intertwined on the center console, and her head bowed in prayer. Though her prayer was more like a whirlwind battle of truths, insecurities, doubts and pleas, through it all, a sliver of peace shone through the tempest in Leanne's heart.

When they finally arrived in Hamilton, they drove straight to the hospital. Leanne could barely keep up with Mike as he hurried through the parking lot. He stopped once to impatiently wait for her to catch up.

Mike entered the ER first, followed shortly by Leanne who slid to a halt at the sight of Karen in the waiting room. She was curled up asleep on Kristina's lap, a bandage over her arm. Rick was oblivious to all that was going on, playing with his cars on the floor near Kristina's feet. Kristina whispered to Mike so as not to wake Karen. "If you go up to the front desk, they'll take you back."

Leanne hugged Rick and shushed his exuberant greetings.

"Grandpa's sick, Mommy. Is he going to be okay?"

From the look in Kristina's eyes, Leanne thought it best not to answer. "The doctors are taking care of him the best they can."

He looked at her for a moment, and then sat back down on the floor to play.

"What happened?" Leanne asked Kristina.

"Andrew collapsed on the kitchen floor – it was his heart. Karen was in there with him." Leanne's hand flew to her mouth as she pictured her daughter's reaction to seeing her grandfather fall to the ground unresponsive. "Her screams brought Sandra in, and they called the paramedics. I guess the sirens and the commotion were so much for her, she started pulling her hair, scratching her skin and biting her arm." Kristina placed her cheek on the top of Karen's head, her mahogany tresses blending with the little girl's blonde curls. A sob ripped from her lips. "She kept saying, 'It's going to be alright, Grandma's kisses will make it better.'"

The two women's tears were interrupted by Nathan, who came back to the waiting room. "He's stable for now, but the doctor doesn't think it looks good." His voice choked on the last words and he struggled to finish. "They are moving him to a room, and then we can go all go in there to see him."

Leanne took Karen from Kristina's lap so the woman could comfort Nathan, who sobbed into his fiancé's arms. There was a gentle strength in Kristina's touch as she held Nathan, and Leanne prayed that she could be that kind of rock for Mike.

As if her thoughts of Mike caused him to materialize, he came into the waiting room, grief etched into every line on his handsome face.

"How's Karen?" Without really looking at her, he touched the top of his daughter's head.

"She's fine. How are you?"

His face mirrored the pain in his heart, but he didn't answer her question. There was a weariness in his voice as Mike explained. "They said Dad might make it through the week – but they also said he might not make it through the night." His last word came out as a stuttered sob, and Leanne wrapped her free arm around his shoulders.

Their hug woke up Karen, and the little girl's smile beamed when she saw her parents. But just as quickly, her smile faded as her sleepy mind came into focus and she remember where she was and why.

Before Leanne could say anything, he took the girl from her and father and daughter cried together for a moment, sharing their pain.

"It's going to be fine." Mike attempted to say, but his words were choked by his sobs.

Leanne knew he said that phrase all the time - to her and to Karen. From the catch in his voice, she could tell he didn't quite believe the words he was saying any more than his daughter did.

Wanting to do something right, something to help him, she said, "Mike, why don't I take the kids home. Give you some time with your dad. I'll come back later this evening."

She saw the look that crossed his face and she wondered if she had chosen the wrong thing to do. But before she could say anything else, Nathan stepped up to them. "Kristina and I can come watch the kids in about an hour so you can come back."

Mike looked uncertain, but after a moment's pause, he nodded his head. She kissed him, brushing the tears from his cheeks. "Call me if...if you need me to come back."

He nodded stiffly and disappeared through the double doors.

Leanne drove home to the sound of silence. As if sensing the mood, Rick was unusually quiet, and Karen simply stared pensively out the window.

Once home, the kids ran inside, each heading to their room without a word. After unpacking the car and their suitcases, Leanne sunk down into the sofa with a weary sigh. Mike's face when she said she was going to take the kids home kept playing over and over in her head. She knew she had somehow disappointed him. She thought she made the right choice. Karen was upset, and Leanne didn't want to disturb everyone and their grief. But his cool goodbye let her know she had once again messed something up.

She was tired of trying to live up to be worthy enough for his love, and too weary to fight against the storms that were pulling her down. Like the woman in the fountain, she had spent their entire relationship trying to plug up the holes she created. Her arms were exhausted from the strain and she was spent from the futility of her attempts.

*God, we learned that You would help us through these storms. Help me, Lord!*

"Mommy?" Leanne looked up to find Karen standing before her, holding out a book for her to read. Gathering her daughter next to her on the couch, Leanne opened the book and began to read.

It was a book Sandra and Andrew had given the kids last Christmas. It was a retelling of the passage from the book of Matthew, chapter eight, when Jesus calmed the storm. Leanne kissed the top of her daughter's golden curls and began to read, the simple sing-song rhyme of the children's book reaching out to her own troubled spirit.

As she turned the last few pages, Leanne read:

*The disciples asked, "Who is this man - the winds and waves obey his word?"*

*That man is Jesus Christ. He came to save us. Or maybe you haven't heard?*

*He loves you. He's full of grace and mercy. He is faithful and He's just.*

*Whether it is a stormy or a sunny day, He is the one you can always trust.*

Leanne closed the simple children's book that had managed to shatter her heart. Earlier, her prayer had come out as a pouting demand to God. Now, her prayer took on a more humbler tone.

*I want to believe you will calm this storm, God. I know what we read last night, and I want to believe it...*

Her words trailed off, and her daughter took the book from her hands. The young girl walked back down the hallway, repeatedly muttering the last page of the book. "Whether it is a stormy or a sunny day, He is the One you can always trust."

Leanne put a shaky hand against her trembling lips. *Please, God. Calm this storm. For her sake, calm this storm.*

The doorbell chimed, and Leanne dashed the wetness from her cheeks.

She opened the door and let Nathan and Kristina in. "How's your dad?"

Nathan just shook his head, fighting back the tears.

Kristina held his hand and spoke for him. "They've got him settled in ICU, and he was resting when we left. But he did have a chance to speak with everyone."

"I'm sorry," or some other worthless triviality sprang to her lips. But she kept it silent. What good would words do now?

"Where are the kids?" Nathan asked after he had reigned in his emotions.

"They are in their rooms right now." Leanne added uncertainly, "Are you sure you want to…I mean, I don't want to take you away from the hospital right now."

Nathan stopped the rest of her sentence. "Leanne, Mike needs you right now. He needs you by his side."

Those words should have been a joyous thing to her, but they rang like a death knoll over and over in her head on the way to the hospital.

Her instinct that she had messed up in her decision to take the kids home wasn't born of her own flagging self-confidence. He had needed her and she took off with the kids. He was always trying to help everyone else out, and when he needed her most, she wasn't there.

When she finally reached the ICU floor, she located the room, but slid to a halt right outside of the door.

She heard Mike's sobbing plea. "Everything is crumbling around me, and I am helpless to do anything about it. I can't fix dad, I can't fix my daughter, and I can't fix my wife...I've tried, but I don't even know how to pull her out of the pit she's in."

She stepped away and ran down the hall to the bathroom. She had heard the defeat and weariness that saturated Mike's voice. Nathan was focused because he didn't have to worry about Kristina. Leanne, on the other hand, was just an added burden to Mike right now.

*Mike needs me, God. So that means I need You! I don't want him to feel like he has to fix me. I just want to help him feel less defeated.* Leanne paused in her prayer and then added, *You are God! You know everything I need and everything he needs. So I guess I don't need to say anything else.*

Praying had always been an awkward ritual she stumbled through with Mike. She had gotten better at it over the years, but it wasn't without practice. But lately, her prayers were silent conversations with God. And though Leanne knew her less-than eloquent prayers would never be written down in children's books or devotionals, they didn't feel awkward to her. As a matter of fact, the more she prayed, the more peace settled into her heart. And if she was going to get through this day, and this dark time with Mike, she was going to need every ounce of peace she could muster.

She headed back down to the room and opened the door with just enough noise to let Mike and his mom know her presence, but at the same time, being careful so she would not disturb Andrew.

When Mike saw her, his arms immediately went around her. *At least he isn't rejecting me.* She held him, silently chanting for God to give him rest.

"What's all this commotion and hugging?"

The sound of Andrew's hoarse voice loosened Mike's hold, and everyone turned to the man lying on the bed.

"Dad," Mike said, coming to his father's side. "We didn't mean to wake you."

"I'm glad you did." Andrew said, and his eyes fell on Leanne. "This beautiful woman came to see me and I aim to have a nice conversation with her." He looked at Mike with a silent plea. "Take your mom down and get her something to eat." When Sandra would have protested, Andrew patted her hand. "Sandy, go take care of yourself."

Leanne could barely suppress her tears at the love she saw shining in the man's blue-gray eyes - eyes so much like his son's.

When everyone had left, Andrew McKinley patted a spot on the bed next to him. Leanne sat down, brushing back the tears that were streaming down her face. Words erupted from her heart, but failed to form on her lips. *Don't leave! You are like the father I needed. You helped erase a lot of pain from my past. You raised a wonderful son. Don't leave me!* But nothing came out, and Leanne just sat there next to Andrew, with tears streaming down her face and falling on their clasped hands. "Andrew..." She began, but the uselessness of her words stung.

"I know what your heart longs to say, but I don't want you to be sad. You have a lot of work to do."

She sniffled. "What do you mean?"

"My son thinks he can fix everything, and I need you to help him understand God is the only one that can fix things."

Her cheeks flamed and she wondered how much of their troubles Mike had shared. "We rededicated our marriage to God. Mike was saying that he thought our foundation was wrong."

"I can see that he understands the truth. But there is a wide chasm between knowing here." His hand trembled as he pointed to his head. "And believing here." Andrew pointed to his heart.

Leanne stared down at him, but her mind was clinging to his words. "But how do I...I mean, how do we cross the chasm?"

Andrew donned a weak smile. He patted her hand. "When you know something in your head only, you want to do that thing, sometimes you even try hard to do that thing. But the chasm is filled with fears, doubts, your own selfish gains, justifications, reasoning, or pride. So when you go to try to do the right thing, it can get swallowed up."

Leanne thought of her own struggle with trusting Mike with the truth of her past. She knew it was the right thing she should do, but her fears and justifications consumed the truth before it was ever breathed.

"And when it gets to your heart?" She asked.

"It is like a seed planted in the ground. You plant the Word of God in your mind, it takes root in your spirit, and the Holy Spirit waters it. You begin to desire it. You can't live without it. You can't breathe without it. It is who you are, and it can't help come out of you in every way."

Leanne's shoulders slumped and she said, "I feel that way as a Christian sometimes. I know what it means to be a Christian. I know how to be a Christian. I know Jesus died on the cross for me, and I know my sins were wiped clean..." Her words trailed off, and she realized she had let all this spill out on a man who might only have hours to live.

But Andrew interrupted her thoughts and the half-formed apologies clamoring to make their escape from her lips. "You need to fall in love."

Leanne's head jerked up at his statement, and Andrew let out a laughed which sputtered into a cough. When he had regained his breath, he said, "You need to fall in love with Jesus. You can't do that until you really know Him. He's not just some historical figure or a concept behind theology. He is *your* personal Savior, and He wants an intimate relationship with you. One that involves letting go of all your preconceived notions about what He is, or what He does. Come to know Him through His word, through your prayers, and through your life, and the lives of other believers. Taking what you know about Him from the Bible, look for the ways He has worked in your life, and you will see Him. You will see His love, you will see His grace, and you will see His mercy. Pretty soon, you'll be able to feel His love, grace and mercy at work in your life, even when chaos has erupted. And when you feel it, you will desire it. You won't be able to live without Him."

Leanne thought that sounded nice, it sounded wonderful, it sounded like something she was hungry for. "I want that."

"I know you do, Leanne." Andrew patted her hand again. "Now I want you to desire it. Let go of your fears, your past, your doubts and justifications, and seek Him out with all of your heart."

"...and you will find Him." Leanne said, remembering a verse her and Mike had read last night.

"Find who?" Mike said, coming through the door on the tail end of their conversation. Concerned tinged his voice. "Do you need me to get the doctor, Dad?"

Leanne rose from his bedside, making room for the family.

"No, Son. Your wife and I were just having a conversation." As if dismissing the whole ordeal, Andrew reached for his wife's hand. "Did you get something to eat, honey?"

"Yes, but I was..."

"Don't say fine. My time might be drawing near, but I don't want to take you with me because you are too busy worrying about what can't be changed. God has his plans."

Sandra lifted her chin, trying to draw strength from his words - from his presence. But Leanne saw Sandra's chin quiver with suppressed sobs. Leanne turned away as her own heart hurt for the woman, for Mike and his brother, and for herself. Andrew McKinley was the kindest, gentlest soul. He had warmly welcomed her into their family over eight years ago, and had graciously dealt with her mother's harping and complaints throughout their wedding. Andrew had said look for evidence of God's grace and mercy in the life of other believers. Andrew McKinley seemed like a great place to start.

# Chapter Nine

*You might be a mechanic, but in the spiritual realm, you are just a tool in the hands of God.*

His father's words echoed through his head as he buttoned up his shirt. A few days ago, his father had mumbled those words to Mike in the hospital room.

The first two weeks after his father's collapse brought a prayerful hope to the McKinley family. The doctor's had not given him more than a week. But when two weeks passed, and Andrew seemed to be improving, hope soared in like a triumphant eagle, giving wings to their prayers.

Last week, he had taken a turn for the worse. Andrew had spoken to him a few days ago. "Son, this family needs you right now. Your mom is going to need you and Nathan to get her through. And Leanne and Karen need you as well. Don't give up on them. They have a rocky journey ahead, but God has placed you in their lives to guide them to Him. Be a reflection of Him and his light, so they will find their way out of the darkness that is closing around them."

Now, Mike stood in front of the dresser in his bedroom, dressed for his father's funeral, and he willed himself to heed his father's words. But there was no strength behind his will, like everything and everyone around him, his strength was crumbling before his eyes, and he felt powerless to stop it.

He was losing his grip on Leanne. Spiritually, she

had made some sort of turn. These past two weeks he had found her with her nose buried in a Bible, pouring over the pages. He was happy to see her seeking God's word, but he could tell she was wrestling with whatever she had found. Leanne looked like a woman caught between conviction and something – and if the dark circles under her eyes were any indication, that *something* was winning.

She had come to him two days ago, seeking solace in his arms after Andrew had died. He doubted the quick pat on her back was sufficient for her.

Mike paused as he tucked the shirt into his suit pants. Maybe he wasn't losing his grip on her, maybe he was just letting her go. He didn't have the strength to support her right now, and that fact alone made the weight around his neck heavier.

Then there was Karen, who was sullen and even more withdrawn than usual. She walked around sucking her thumb and rubbing her ear in worry. But it was her eyes that tore at him. Her brow was often furrowed deep in thought, and she looked at them as if trying to discern something greater than her age...greater than *their* age. The night before Andrew had died, Mike had walked by Karen's room to find her rocking on her bed, tears streaming down her face, singing her favorite Bible song.

*It's me, it's me, oh Lord,*

*Standing in the peanut bread.*

*Not my mother, not my father,*

*But it's me oh Lord,*

*Standing in the peanut bread.*

Usually the song made them laugh because she would say, *standing in the peanut bread* instead of *need of prayer*. But tonight it was different. Despite her mangling of the lyrics, she understood the heart of the song. She rocked and sang to a God she was hoping would save her grandfather. She was crying out to a God who she'd been told hears our prayers. But preschool Sunday school classes don't cover unanswered prayers, God's timing, and God's overall purpose and plan, which supersedes ours. They don't prepare a four-year-old for the death of a grandfather.

Mike had gone in and rocked her until she'd fallen asleep. He hadn't known what else to do. She wasn't an inconsolable six-month-old with teething issues. She wasn't a feverish two-year-old who just needed soothing until the medicine kicked in. But she was a very sad and troubled girl who had a pain in her spirit that he couldn't fix. After he put her to bed, he curled up next to Leanne in their own bed. Wrapping an arm around her waist, he pulled her close to him. She turned in his arms and held him. They had fallen asleep like that, him praying that he could fix those he loved, all the while wishing someone would come along and fix him.

And now he stood before the mirror, shrugging the black suit jacket over his pale pink shirt, preparing to bury his father. The man who guided him whenever he was lost was now gone, and he had never felt more adrift in his problems.

Tears burned the back of his eyes. *Dad, I don't know what to do. And now you aren't here to ask.*

Leanne walked into the room. She paused for a moment of uncertainty and he could tell that she was trying to gauge his tears, his mood, and what she should do about them. She must have decided to forage ahead despite her fears. He felt like a heel for his impatience with his wife lately. But he didn't have enough strength to stand up on his own weary legs, let alone carry her, too.

Memory of the illustration they went through at the Triple R Resort surfaced for a brief second, but the weight of his sadness dragged it down before it could change his attitude. It was with that exhausted impatience he noticed she was still dressed in her gray sweats and white long sleeved t-shirt that she was wearing this morning.

"You're not dressed?"

Confusion marred her beautiful features. "I thought we said we weren't going to take the kids?"

He remembered the conversation. It was more like a worn-down attempt at an argument. He had wanted to take the kids and give them a chance to say goodbye, but she had argued about Karen's difficulty already with Andrew's death. Despite his feelings, he had caved when she said, "Besides, I want you to have a chance to grieve without worrying about her. I want a chance to do that as well. Andrew was more to me than just my father-in-law…" Her tears ended the conversation. He was too drained to fight, too frustrated to concede, and too irked to console her. He had just left the room.

Mike turned back to the mirror and adjusted his tie. "I assumed you were going to find someone to watch them?"

"Everyone had plans to attend the funeral." She wiped her hands nervously on her pants. "I can have the kids ready if you want us all to go?"

Mike shook his head. His voice was flat. "No. Just stay home with them."

"Mike..." she began, but the doorbell interrupted her.

Mike coolly brushed past her and headed toward the front of the house. He opened the door to see one of Nathan's high school students with a baby carrier. "Barbara, what are you doing here?"

"Kristina and Nathan said you were looking for someone to watch the kids during the funeral. I didn't want to go and bring Amari, so I offered to watch your kids." She looked past Mike at Leanne's attire. "Didn't you get Kristina's message?"

"My phone must have been on silent. I turned the ringer off at the hospital the other day."

"Well, if you all don't mind Amari and me hanging out with the kids, I'd be glad to watch Karen and Rick for you."

Mike looked at Leanne, thinking she'd have a million reasons not to trust Barbara. He was surprised to see her nod her head and then rush off to get changed.

The drive to the church was done in complete

silence, something that had become a norm between the two of them.

She reached for his hand as she had many times over their marriage. He wanted to feel good about her presence next to him, but a tendril of impatience coiled through his heart. He had wanted her by his side at the hospital, but she had gone home with the kids. He had wanted the kids at the funeral, but she had hidden them away. With a sigh and a sharp pang of guilt, he surreptitiously slipped his hand out from under hers to grip the steering wheel.

He was hurt, angry, and...

Mike searched his heart to name the feeling that he had been dragging around lately. Lost and alone - that is how he felt. For the first time in their marriage, he was lost and alone, without the strength to encourage her. He needed her strength, but he knew she didn't have it to give.

As they arrived at the church, he should have been happy that she was at his side. She seemed to be trying to offer herself up as a crutch to lean on, but her support was clinging to him like a static-ridden shirt. The more he tried to pull on it, the more it adhered to him.

The funeral was longer than expected, as church members and friends alike got up to speak of how much Andrew McKinley touched their lives. Mike was proud of his younger brother, who managed to officiate the service despite his grief. Leanne cried quietly next to him, and he placed his arm around her. She reached for his other hand, squeezing it in a gesture of support. He smiled a two-dimensional smile down at her, willing it to have more depth, more feeling - but he felt numb inside.

When she turned to embrace his mom after the service, he felt bad for the sense of relief it brought him.

"Why don't you go get the kids and bring them by the house, Mike?" Sandra said later as they left the cemetery.

"Karen won't like all the noise and commotion." Hearing his wife's usual excuses come out of his own mouth gave him pause.

"Oh, I guess you're right." Sadness flickered over her face. "It was something we loved sharing...being grandparents that is." Her words trailed off in tears, and Mike wrapped his arms around his mom's shuddering shoulders.

"It's going to be okay, Mom." Mike thought about how Leanne said his platitudes didn't fix anything. Nothing he did could fix this emptiness gnawing at him.

Pulling back, he tried to shake himself out of his mood. "Leanne and I can drop by tomorrow with the kids. We will spend the day with you."

Sandra just nodded her head, unable to speak through her tears.

The rest of the day went by in a whirlwind of condolences, memories, and hugs. Through it all, Leanne tried to be by his side or Sandra's. He wanted to remember to thank her for it later, but he wasn't sure he would. There was a fog about him, and a heavy weight that made his steps seem like too much of an effort to take.

At one point, in an attempt to escape it all, he shut himself in his father's study. Leaning back in the leather chair, he looked around at the shelves lined with Bibles and books. He could read all the words encased in the works of room and still not have the wisdom his father had.

Mike rested his elbows on the desk and buried his face in his hands, giving way to his tears. *I need him, God!* Mike silently railed. *I need him, and You took him from me!*

After his tears subsided, he wiped the moisture from his face and used his sleeve to mop up the small puddles on the desk. He opened the drawers, looking for a box of tissues. As he lifted the box out of the drawer, his eyes fell on his dad's prayer journal that was underneath it.

Pulling it out, he laid it on the desk and ran his hand across the leather bound cover. He remembered passing by this office door every morning to see his dad's head bent, a steaming cup of coffee on one side of him, his Bible open on the other side.

Mike wanted to open it. He wanted to seek comfort in the whispered prayers of his father over the years. Instead, Mike picked it up and went in search of his mom and brother.

"Hey, Mike, how are you holding up?" Nathan asked as he came into the kitchen. Most of the guests were gone, and just a few close friends and family remained.

Mike shrugged. "I found this in dad's desk."

Sandra came to stand beside Nathan. With a trembling hand she reached out for the book. "His prayer journal." Just shy of grasping the book, Sandra turned from them. "You two can have it. I don't think I could…"

Leanne was the first to reach for Sandra and wrap her in a hug as the matron of the family sobbed into Leanne's shoulder. "I tried to prepare. I knew he wasn't going to make it. So why does it still hurt so much?"

Mike wrapped his arms around both his mom and his wife. He tried to summon his inner Andrew McKinley. "I know, Mom. I think it is going to hurt us all for a while."

Nathan stepped up and added. "Whenever we were torn apart by some sort of storm in our life, Dad would always make us gather together, hold hands, and pray. He always said, 'When life hits you so hard you can barely see in front of you…"

Sandra and Mike joined in to finish the statement. "'…close your eyes and seek the God above you."

The group made a small circle in the kitchen, with Kristina and Leanne flanking the men, and Sandra sandwiched between her sons. Nathan began as they all grasped each other's hands.

"Heavenly Father, we thank you for giving us the wonderful support we have in each other and in Your word. I know the days and the weeks ahead are going to be tough for each of us. We will have our separate struggles, Lord, but You know what those are."

Nathan's prayer was choked with tears. "Dad's always been there, and I am not sure how to operate in a world without him."

Mike's tears plopped on the kitchen tile unheeded as his brother echoed the sadness of his own heart.

"Lord, as we surround my mother with love and support, I ask you to surround her with Your peace. I know an ounce of Your peace is better than anything we could give her."

With a shaky indrawn breath, Nathan finished his prayer. "Surround Mike and I with a little of that peace as well, and strength to help not only Mom, but our own family, too."

Nathan's prayer stung his conscience and encouraged him all at the same time. Wrapping an arm about Leanne's shoulder, he kissed the top of her head.

As the prayer ended, the group agreed to come together again for breakfast and spend the day together tomorrow. As they were heading out the kitchen door, Mike heard Kristina ask Leanne. "How is Karen doing?"

"She is missing her Grandpa. I don't think she quite understands that he's gone." Leanne's hand fluttered to the side in a gesture of defeat. "I don't know how to explain that…"

Kristina's arm encircled his wife's shoulders. "I don't think there is an easy way, but you are a great mom. If anyone can handle this, you will do it flawlessly."

Mike saw the pleasure Kristina's comment drew

from Leanne.

*I know that should be me encouraging her, God. But I'm just so tired.*

# Chapter Ten

Leanne stared silently out the car window, lost in her own thoughts.

The next morning had dawned with no change to the indifferent existence that their marriage had become. If there was a fissure between them before Andrew's death, now there was an abyss. She clung desperately to the side, not wanting to fall in, but Mike seemed content to just slip through.

They had arrived that morning at Sandra's house for breakfast, and Leanne watched as Mike and Nathan surrounded Sandra McKinley with a carefully balanced dose of sweet memories and laughter, bathed in love and silent prayer. Kristina seemed to have this inner strength that buoyed her up from the sadness surrounding the family, and allowed her to support Nathan.

Leanne felt her efforts at comfort were bungled attempts that left Mike doing more of the consoling than her.

Later in the afternoon, Sandra had given each of the brothers a spiral bound book. "Your father began writing this the moment we found out I was pregnant with you, Mike." Brushing away the tears, Sandra continued. "It's a collection of his thoughts, memories…" Her voice trailed off into a brief sob, and she sniffled. "Well, you know how he was. It was like his own version of a scrapbook."

Leanne watched as Mike hesitantly opened it up.

He hadn't read far when he closed it, quietly stood and walked out of the house.

As she sat there, debating on whether to give him space or go after him, Nathan followed him out the door. She hated her insecurities and self-doubt. They had kept her bound up all her life. She should be the one out there with her husband.

Rick climbed into her lap, and she buried her burning cheeks in his hair, refusing to look up at the other women in the room.

But her self-involved thoughts of her own stupidity was quickly eclipsed when Sandra rose to go to the kitchen when the men returned.

"No, Grandma!" Karen's screams filled the house as the little girl raced toward Sandra, pulling on her arm and preventing her from entering the kitchen.

Mike came running in, and was at Karen's side before Leanne could reach her. Scooping his daughter up, Mike rocked her soothingly. Mike looked at Leanne for answers, but she didn't miss the flicker of frustration in his eyes when he looked at her.

*He can't even go outside and grieve. He has to come in to help his daughter, and from the look in his eyes, he clearly thinks I'm not capable of helping her.*

"Karen, Grandma is just going to get some cookies for everyone." Sandra said, taking a few steps toward the kitchen.

Leanne came to Mike's side, attempting to help him as their daughter thrashed about wildly in his arms, seeking escape from his hold. Their attempts to console her were useless.

"Baby, come here." Sandra took their daughter into her arms, and sat down with her on the couch. Karen clung tightly to her neck.

When she had settled down, Sandra asked. "Do you want to come with me to the kitchen?"

Karen became distraught again, vigorously shaking her head no. The little girl finally found her voice. "I don't want you to fall down and die like Grandpa."

A hush had settled over the room as the adults gained an understanding that left them heartbroken. Leanne pressed a trembling hand to her lips to cover her cry.

"What are we going to do?" Mike's voice pulled her from her reminiscences. Leanne turned from the car window to stare at him as he drove.

"She has her test in a couple of weeks." It was her best answer, as lame as it was. Glancing in the back seat to make sure she was asleep, Leanne whispered. "Mike, do you think she blames herself?"

She saw the tears pool at the bottom of his eyes and he blinked them away. "I don't know."

He repeated it again, this time in a softer tone that held even less hope for her.

Leanne turned toward the window again. The overwhelming sadness that gripped her husband left her, a woman who walked from one helpless level to another, clueless as to what to do.

*I guess this is Your way of testing our foundation.* She accused God. Less than a month ago, they had held hands and declared to God they were going to strengthen their marriage. That next day, it was as if God was hurtling circumstances their way to prove how false their statements were.

Her lower lip trembled as she pouted silently. *We are flooded with troubles. How are we supposed to stand in the midst of all this rain?*

After they got the kids in bed, she came up to him in their room. He was standing with his back to her, his head hanging down. She wrapped her arms around his waist and kissed him between his shoulder blades. Leanne didn't know how to comfort him any other way, but she hoped that her closeness could help ease his suffering a little.

He turned toward her and held her face tenderly in his hand. He kissed her as if he was giving her breath, and she returned the kiss as if trying to outdo his comfort.

He pulled back and brushed her cheeks with his thumbs.

She started to reach up and pull his head down for another kiss, but something in eyes held her at bay.

"Mike?" His name was both a plea and a question.

He placed soft kisses along her brow. A gesture he had done so many times before, but tonight they seemed sweeter to her than usual.

Her name came out in a pained whisper. "Leanne, I love you."

She kissed away his words. She was trying to be the best wife she knew how to be. She couldn't be a pillar of strength like Sandra had always been for

Andrew. She couldn't even be the quiet strength that Kristina was for Nathan. But she prayed that her kisses, her touch, her love could be enough to ease the pain that was etched into every handsome line on her husband's face.

Mike gently gripped her arms and pulled her back a little. The weariness of his voice cut her to the quick. "Leanne, I love you, but not tonight."

He turned and headed to the bathroom, leaving a stunned Leanne in his wake.

As the next week wore on, there was little change in the atmosphere of their house. The more distant Mike became, the more she sought to please him, but her efforts were always met with the same weary apologies.

Two weeks after his father's funeral, Leanne was frantic to have her old husband back. As Mike put the kids to bed, she pulled out her most enticing nightgown.

She heard the phone ring while she was in the bathroom getting changed, and when she came out, she found Mike standing there with the phone in his hand.

Encouraged by the look that crossed his face at the sight of her, though part of her thought she saw regret scamper across his features, Leanne came to stand before him. Taking the phone from his hand, she tossed it on the bed and wound her arms around his neck.

He didn't resist her kisses, though he didn't exactly respond whole-heartedly, either. When he lifted his head, her name as a gentle whisper. That was enough encouragement for her, and she would have redoubled her seduction, if it wasn't for his restraining hands on her arms.

"Please, Mike." She cried, as tears coursed down her cheeks at being rejected by him again. "I am trying my best to support you, love you, and be what you need right now."

"Leanne..."

Fear that her marriage was destined to be the cold lifeless entity that it had become spurred her words on, unheeded and unchecked by reason. "Mike, I don't know how to be Sandra or Kristina! I don't know how to be perfect like my sisters. But I know how to do this, please, let me do this."

Mike stared down at her for a moment, confusion knitting his brow. After a moment, he shook his head. "Leanne, your stepfather was killed in a car wreck tonight."

Leanne stared up at him for a few moments as she processed his words. She shook out of his loosely held restraint to wind her arms around his neck and she kissed him with a fervor.

"Leanne!" Mike pulled away from her kisses. "Did you hear me?"

Threading her fingers through his hair, she whispered. "Yes, I heard you."

He stared down at her, and she knew he was looking for some sort of reaction from her. "I don't want to call her back right now. I just want to focus on you – on us! You have been through so much lately…"

He pulled back from her as if she disgusted him. He raked his hand down his face and fairly screamed, "Sex isn't going to help me get over my father any more than avoiding your mother is going to make your stepfather's funeral any easier to deal with."

She cut him off. "I'm not going to the funeral." She knew she was getting into dangerous territory right now, but everything was crumbling anyway. There wasn't enough strength inside her to playact through his funeral.

"If it's the kids, you know I can watch them while you go…"

"It isn't the kids. I just need to be here for you and Karen right now."

Anxiety crept up along the back of her neck, and she hoped her words would placate this turbulent conversation. But his next words disabused her of any such notion.

"Leanne, I know your mom did and said a lot to hurt you. But she needs you right now."

Anger boiled up in her at his words, and before she could contain them, her comment rushed out. "What about me! I needed her when she let him…"

Taking a few steady breaths, she tuned from Mike trying to get herself under control.

When she had regulated her emotions, she turned back to him. If he wanted her to go, she would. The way he was looking at her now was what she always feared – like he saw her for who she really was, and he didn't like what he saw. To placate him, she would keep up appearances. She could endure the funeral.

"I'll go."

Mike pulled her gently in his arms, thinking she needed comfort. When he reached out for her, she accepted his touch. Moments ago, she would have given anything for his kisses. Now, she allowed him to kiss her, to touch her – but only because she needed him. If she turned him away, he might never come back.

Leanne put on her best Lee-Lee act, and let her husband take her in his arms, carry her to the bed, and make love to her. And when he had finally fallen asleep, that is when she escaped to the bathroom.

She turned on the shower to mask her tears. Bracing her hands on the counter, she gave full vent to all of her carefully controlled emotions that she had worked so hard to keep in check over these years of marriage.

*Enough*! She screamed at God. *What do you want from me? How many times do I have to say I'm sorry? I have been a good wife. I have gone to church and prayed with my family. I help out in the nursery every other Sunday, and...*

Her prayer swirled away like the water coursing down the drain in the shower as she stepped under the steamy spray. She wanted to wash these past few hours away. She wanted to wash so many things away. For once, she wanted to be clean. Clean from her past, her lies, and the filth that stained every inch of her life.

But she had done what Andrew McKinley said. She had spent time in God's word, and she was beginning to know Him.

*Don't ask me to tell Mike the truth.* She pleaded with God. *I know that is what You want, but how can that be a good thing? How is he going to react?*

Resting her head against the cool tile wall, she let her tears fall silently. Yesterday, she had been reading the Psalms. The writer was begging God to hear his prayer, and Leanne struggled to remember the words of the first verse in Psalm four. "Answer me when I call to you, O God who declares me innocent. Free me from my troubles. Have mercy on me and hear my prayer."

She wanted to cry out those words to God, but her voice stilled. *I'm not innocent.*

# Chapter Eleven

"Hello, Mike, is Leanne there?" Lacey's voice was tinged with equal parts weariness and frustration.

"I thought she was with you all?" Mike sat up on the couch. "She left two days ago for the funeral."

Silence stretched across the line as Mike's imagination danced across his mind, conjuring images of her wrecked along the side of the road, stranded, or worse.

"She called this morning and said she couldn't make it after all. I just assumed something happened with Karen."

Mike was silent for a moment, before jumping up from the couch. "I will call you back as soon as I get a hold of her."

As he listened to her cell phone ring, he was trying to come up with a plausible reason for her lies. But no matter how he twisted or turned the facts, there was no configuration that made sense. And with each moment, his anger burned and his frustration with his wife increased.

"Leanne, I don't know where you are and what you are doing, but give me a call the second you get this."

He began pacing back and forth, but stopped when Rick laughed and took up step beside him.

Hitting upon a reasonable excuse, he nursed it to keep his imagination at bay. Maybe she had gone, but decided against it, turned around and was heading back home. Leanne was always forgetting to turn her cell phone back off silent mode.

Yet, with each passing hour, and no return call from her, he began to wonder more and more about the likelihood of his fabricated explanation.

*Affair*, skipped across his brain a time or two, but he wrestled it down. Not Leanne. She was always with him and clung to him.

His traitorous imagination reminded him of how she always turned to the physical side of their relationship. It was how she solved everything, how she showed her emotions…

*I know how to do this, please, let me do this.* Her seductive plea the other night tortured him, reminding him of how cold he had been to her. Struggling under the weight of his father's death, he had ignored her, been impatient with her. Had she turned to someone else?

*No!* He couldn't believe she would do that, so he left her another voice message and a text message to eradicate the thought.

Rest would not come so easily to his mind, however. Her awkward statements, her needy personality, her intense sexual drive over the years of their marriage played over and over in his head.

In another attempt to quiet his thoughts, he prayed. *God, please let her be okay.*

The sound of keys in the door sent him leaping from the couch.

"Where have you been?"

Her face paled at his thunderous tone.

Before she could answer, he railed on. "I thought you were going to the funeral. But you lied!"

Maybe it was his pent up emotions from his father's death and his concerns with Karen. Maybe it was the hours his imagination had been given freedom to roam. Maybe it was a combination of all of those things. Mike had never raised his voice so harshly to her in their eight years of marriage. The result was a quivering chin and a whispered, "I'm sorry" from Leanne.

He tried to calm his voice, but his anger was still mounted and riding through his mind. "I was worried sick. Your sister called wondering where you were. And here I am, thinking you are with her."

When she didn't say anything, he continued. "I thought you were lying on the side of the road somewhere in an accident." He was pacing back and forth again in front of her downcast face. "I thought you might be dead."

Mike stopped in front of her, leaning down as he choked out in a whispered sob. "I thought you were having an affair."

At this, she looked up. Her face held some unnamed emotion, and Mike was sure he had hit a nerve. *Was it the truth?*

"Mike, I would never."

He sighed in relief, but his anger was no less abated by her words. "Then tell me what happened?"

"I couldn't go."

He stood before her, hands on his hips, trying to make sense of this resentment she had toward her mother. While he had no doubt Deborah was a difficult woman to grow up with, he also knew Leanne was a peacemaker. He had fallen in love with her forgiving nature, her gentle grace and the mercy which she so freely gave to everyone - everyone but her mother.

When he was in high school, he had a girlfriend who he cared about deeply, but when Laura didn't get her way, or others wronged her, she had no qualms about letting them know. Though she was sweet and loving toward him, there was always an air of conflict about her.

So when he met Leanne, he was enchanted by her quiet and gentle nature. When Nathan had been struggling with one of his youth students a couple of years ago, she had been the one to remind everyone the boy was more than his actions, and to look beyond what he was doing to see what the heart of his troubles were. When Mrs. Rose had gruffly overtaken a ladies' luncheon, Leanne was the only one who had approached her with kindness. Even when a woman in the store the other day made a thoughtless and unkind remark about Karen's behavior, Leanne had turned the other cheek.

Over their eight years of marriage, Leanne had taught him not just to look at things from the other person's shoes, but to look at them through their eyes and with their emotions.

Yet, when it came to her mother, Leanne was ridged in her refusal of forgiveness.

"Can we talk about it after the kids go to bed?"

He looked down at her, her long blonde hair hung down as she refused to look at him, obscuring her face.

Mike ran a hand through his hair in frustration. "Sure."

She looked up briefly when he went to take her suitcase to the room. Shaking her head, she whispered. "Leave it out, just in case."

She brushed past him and went to speak with the kids. He leaned against the living room wall, watching her smile at the kids. But he could see that the smile didn't reach her eyes, and her hugs were a little too long and too tight for normal reunions.

Mike felt as if someone had pulled on a thread in their marriage, and it was all starting to unravel. *What did she mean, just in case? Is she leaving me?*

A sense of anxiety and doom settled into his heart as he struggled to get through the rest of the evening. He caught her staring at him once at dinner, and the look of longing filled her eyes, while uncertainty set her lips in a grim line.

*Whatever it is, Leanne, we can get through this.* He tried to silently convey that to her in a look, but she quickly averted her eyes.

Guilt sagged her shoulders, and it was the resigned acceptance of that guilt which scared him the most. She had denied having an affair, but what else could she be guilty of?

His mind raced over the possibilities, hurdling them one by one, until he landed on the only possibility that he dared to entertain. She felt guilty that she hadn't attended her father's funeral.

He held tightly to that belief, trying to massage it into life. He clung to it as they tucked the kids into bed, though the assumption wriggled to be free. And, in defeat, he let it scamper out of the room when she sat on the bed, tears coursing down her cheeks.

Kneeling before her, he reached to brush the tears from her face, but she stilled his hands.

"No, Mike, I don't deserve your gentle touch."

"Leanne, I don't know what is going on, but it doesn't matter. I love you no matter what."

Those words elicited a sob from her. Again, she averted her eyes. "I don't know how to begin."

He sat down on the bed next to her and tried to grasp her hand. She scooted back to the middle of the bed, tucking her legs underneath her, and folded her hands in her lap.

"Before he died, your dad talked to me about the difference between knowing God in our head, and knowing Him in our heart. He said that when I knew God in my heart, when I fell in love with Him, I would begin to desire His will in my life over everything else."

Mike tried again to reach for her hand, but she eluded his grasp.

"I don't know if I am at that point, yet." Leanne tucked a strand of hair behind her ear. "But I know I have been having a hard time justifying things anymore."

"Justifying what?"

"My lies."

Mike stood up slowly at her words. "What lies?"

Her lower lip trembled as she struggled to get the words out through her tears.

"Our whole marriage is built on lies, or omissions – it's the same thing, I guess." The tears that were pooling in her ice blue eyes ran in twin rivulets down her cheeks as she whispered. "I'm so sorry, Mike."

He ran a hand through his hair. He was torn between comforting her and wanting to hear the truth. Her tears were breaking his heart and the pain and anguish on her face made him want to gather her in his arms. But at the same time, she still hadn't answered him about the lies.

She looked away from him again, and he had to strain to hear her words. "I know you thought I was a Christian when we married, but I just wanted to spend as much time with you as possible. So when you asked me to come to church with you..." Leanne shrugged her shoulders before she continued, "I said yes."

Relief seeped through his tense shoulders at her words.

"I have been reading the Bible, and I know what it says about being unevenly yoked. I put you in that position, and you thought otherwise..."

Her words trailed off at his chuckle. "Leanne, we may have been unevenly yoked, but it seems to me you are truly coming to know Christ now."

Pulling her off the bed, he gathered her in his arms, trailing kisses along her brow. "My love, you should have told me." He rested his cheek against her soft hair and added, "You could have told me." He thought about his attitude lately, and said, "But maybe I didn't make it easy for you to speak up."

She tried to pull back, but he crushed her to him, not wanting to let her go. All the emotions and fears that were twisting his heart a moment ago were washed away with relief that it was something simple they could easily rectify. For a brief moment, he had felt his marriage crumbling under his feet. He held her tightly, breathing in the scent of her hair as if it were the finest fragrance.

After a few moments, he pulled back a tad and cupped her face in his hands. "Leanne, I love you. That's unconditional. Don't ever hesitate to tell me anything."

He bent his head and captured her mouth in a tender kiss. He briefly felt her resistance, but it was a mere breath of hesitation. She kissed him back, and he tasted her tears. She lifted on her toes to deepen the kiss, but her hands hung near her side.

She broke free with a sob.

Somewhere in the back of his mind, he registered the fact that she pulled away, that she wasn't holding him and responding to him like she usually did. But that was in the back of his mind – but at the forefront of his thoughts was the sweet realization that he wasn't losing her. Mike cupped her beautiful face in his hands again. "Leanne, you scared me." He brushed his thumbs across her cheeks, marveling in their softness, treasuring what he had seconds ago thought he had lost.

"Mike…"

He trailed kisses across her cheeks, and then he tried to capture her lips again.

Just shy of their mark, she pleaded in a tearful whisper. "Stop, Mike."

He pulled back, looking down at her. *Thank you, God! I don't know what I would have done without her.*

She stepped out of his embrace, and the look on her face sent the feeling of impending doom flooding back into his heart.

"I shouldn't have let you kiss me." Her trembling fingers went to her lips to quiet the sob that threatened to burst through. It escaped despite her efforts.

He thought he had dodged a bullet, but from her angst-ridden face, he knew she must have been easing into it. And when she spoke next, Mike felt like a trap door had opened up beneath him, plummeting him down from a floor he'd been standing securely on a second ago.

"Mike, I'm not done."

## Chapter Twelve

Leanne had thought easing into her confessions would make it easier on Mike, but from the look on Mike's face, she knew she had caused him more grief. Now she had to come clean. The truth would either bring them together, or tear them apart.

As much as she wanted to rest back in the security of his arms, she had to tell him if they were ever going to have a truly successful marriage.

As she sat in her hotel room last night, she had opened the Bible. She had been scouring it for weeks, trying to find a reason to keep quiet about her past, but what she found was an ever-present gnawing in the pit of her stomach. She clung to the Scriptures about God's grace and mercy. She rested in the picture of God as a fortress, a place of refuge. And she wanted to grasp tightly to the idea of freedom – freedom from her sins, her past, and her lies.

But freedom came with repentance from her sins. Though she had cried out to God for forgiveness, she felt this nudge within her to come clean to her husband. Like a piece of popcorn stuck between her teeth, the idea of confessing her lies to Mike prodded her all day. The more she tried to reason and justify why it could only hurt him more, the deeper that popcorn kernel wedged into her gums.

Now she stood before him and whispered the ninth and tenth verses of Psalm nine.

"The Lord is a shelter for the oppressed, a refuge

in times of trouble. Those who know your name trust in you, for you, O Lord, do not abandon those who search for you."

In the moment she had read that Scripture, she had packed her bags and headed back to Hamilton - back to her husband who deserved the truth. And though she didn't know what consequences her revelation would have, she knew she was tired. Once she had made her decision, that gnawing feeling dissipated. Her heart still hurt as her fears of the outcomes ricocheted against its walls, but she had found peace. A peace she had sought her whole life.

With an inward sigh, she thought, *Here we go, God.*

Mike had not moved in her silence as he waited expectantly for her to finish.

"I brought up my lack of faith in the beginning of our relationship not so much as a confession, but so you can understand. I want you to know that I honestly kept this from you because, in my flawed thinking, I believed that I would just hurt you by revealing the truth. But God has shown me that this isn't just the source of my own troubles, but the source of some of the problems in our marriage."

Leanne saw his brow furrow, but he said nothing.

"I let you believe you were my first, like I was yours." She peeked at him, seeing the pain slash across his face.

"Obviously, you now know that's not true."

She watched him visibly struggle to say something. She knew Mike well enough to know he was trying to say it would be okay, to try to brush it off as the past. But from his pursed lips, the words must have tasted foul on his lips.

"The reason I've never wanted the kids to go to my mom's house, and the reason I didn't want to attend Russell's funeral, wasn't because of my mom."

She couldn't look at him anymore, because she didn't want to see the look of disgust that would cross his face at her next revelation. "My stepfather sexually abused me when I turned sixteen until I was eighteen. The only reason he left me alone after that was because I ended up pregnant. I had kept it a secret and I had planned to run away after graduation. But one night, I hemorrhaged, and he was the one to find me."

His silence cut her to the core, but she knew her secret had left him with little to say.

"Look, Mike. I know you probably hate me for the lies. I tried to be a good wife to you. I tried to love you and be worthy of your love. But I don't think I ever really knew how to do that."

"I don't..." Mike's voice was as soft as a breath of wind. "I don't hate you."

Leanne would have loved to feel his arms around her. She felt so alone standing there in the middle of their bedroom. On the drive back from Albuquerque, she had prayed that he would just crush her to him and say, "I understand your pain and why you lied. But I love you, and we can work through anything."

But he stood three feet from her, his hands clenched at his sides, his face stricken. Moments earlier, he had brushed away her tears, confessing his unconditional love.

Now she could tell he was struggling with what he knew he should do, and what he wanted to do, which was walk away from her.

She'd make it easy for him.

"I'll go."

"No!" He reached out a hand to stop her, but his hand fell short of actually touching her. Despite this, hope blossomed within her chest, but quickly wilted at his next words. "I'll stay at my mom's. You should be with the kids."

She nodded, her vision blurred by her tears. She stumbled to the door, unable to bear his stony silence.

"Leanne." She turned to look at him and her heart broke. He looked so lost and helpless. She wanted to tell him she was sorry again, but she knew the words were worthless at this point.

Mike began again, "Leanne, I just need some time to sort through all of this. It's not that..." His words trailed off, and she nodded as if she understood.

But she didn't understand, or at least she didn't want to have to understand. She wanted that unconditional love he had promised moments ago – but that was before she revealed her dirty past.

"Just give me time to sort through all the questions I have running through my mind right now."

Leanne nodded again, not trusting her voice.

She headed toward the office, closing the door behind her. The sight of him walking out the door wasn't something she could bear right now.

Sitting down in the chair, she leaned her elbows on the top of the desk and buried her face in her hands. She wanted to rail at God. She wanted to scream at Him, *Look at what You have done!* But despite the outcome, she had a sense of peace. It wasn't an easy peace to swallow, but it was the first time in a long while that she felt certain of a choice she made.

Since Russell had started sneaking into her room, Leanne couldn't remember a time when she wasn't engulfed in pain and darkness. Even after she married Mike, that darkness lurked in every corner, threatening to swallow her up in its gloomy depths.

But Leanne finally felt like she was standing on solid ground, and even though she felt like everything around her was tumbling into the abyss, she was confident she wouldn't be pulled under. She had peace in the midst of pain, and a sense of God's purpose and presence in her life, despite the fact that it looked otherwise.

She lifted her chin, which was trembling with suppressed tears, and whispered the second verse to Psalm sixty-two. "He alone is my rock and my salvation, my fortress where I will never be shaken."

# Chapter Thirteen

Mike closed the car door, resting his wrist across the steering wheel. A part of him wanted to go back inside. Driving away from his wife and his family wasn't something he thought he would ever do.

But he didn't know how to process everything, and he didn't want to risk hurting Leanne even more than she had already been hurt.

His own pain and his own anger would trip him up.

He slammed the flat of his hand against the steering wheel and finally gave into his tears. Pictures from their past came flying back into his mind, and the clarity that the recently revealed truth brought to those pictures made him want to scream.

He remembered Leanne standing stiffly next to her stepfather when he had first brought her car back to her. He had thought her reserved smile had been attributed to her shy nature.

Her unexpected burst of anger when he had teasingly called her Lee-Lee, her stepfather's nickname for her. He felt a batch of vile rising in his throat at what that name must have meant to her. *And it came from my lips!*

The way she had always tried to please him sexually, as if that was the only value she brought to him. *Russell taught her that*, he thought as a sob tore through him. That man had stripped her of her innocence and her value.

Mike slammed the car into reverse and peeled out of the driveway, heading to his mother's house. It was a good thing Russell was dead, because the anger surging through him right now would have led him straight to the Bryant household.

"Son, what are you doing here?" Sandra looked behind him, expecting to see his family.

"I need to stay here tonight."

Sandra stepped aside without question and closed the door behind him. Setting his suitcase down, he wrapped his mom in a fierce hug. Just a couple of weeks ago, he had cried on her shoulder about the death of his father. Now he was crying because he felt like his marriage had also died. No, he corrected himself, not his marriage, but everything they stood on had crumbled out from underneath him tonight. Now he no longer knew where he stood, or if he could ever get back.

When his tears had subsided, he picked up his suitcase and headed toward the guest room. He could feel his mother's eyes on him, but knew she wouldn't press him for answers tonight.

Falling back on the bed, he kicked off his shoes and stared up at the ceiling.

Tears coursed down his temples and pooled in his ears. He sat up and swiped at his tears, as if they were the source of all his troubles.

*Dad, I wish you were here. I know you'd have some words of wisdom for me.*

The empty room didn't respond to his request. Deep within his spirit, he knew that guidance from his father was silver, but God's words were gold.

Sniffling, he swiped at his nose and then reached for the Bible on the nightstand.

*Guide me, God.*

The pages of the Bible rustled and crackled as he turned and flipped through God's Word throughout the night. Mike sought answers, but his troubled heart was so jumbled with emotions, he didn't even know the questions he sought answers for. Sometime in the middle of the night, he had finally fallen asleep with his head resting on the Bible.

The sun was reaching its arms in a languid stretch over the horizon when Mike was jolted awake.

After a quick shower, he joined his mom in the kitchen.

"How are you this morning?"

He accepted the cup of coffee she offered him, taking time before he answered her question. "Okay."

Sandra turned back to the stove and added. "I was glad to hear the sound of Bible pages turning all night long. Did you find some answers?"

Mike didn't reply at first, taking a moment to sip the coffee and formulate his answer. "Yes and no."

She banged the spatula on the side of the pan, clearing it of the scrambled eggs that clung to it, before setting it down. "Did you find peace?"

Tears threatened to burst through. "I don't know if I can ever have peace again."

Sandra turned toward him, rubbing her hand on her son's shoulder in comfort. "Nonsense, peace comes from knowing who God is, not from circumstances."

"You don't understand, Mom."

Sandra cut him off. "Don't tell me there is something out there in this entire universe, which God created, that is greater than Him."

"It's not that simple, Mom."

"Do I have to say 'nonsense' again?" Sandra's tone elicited a small chuckle from Mike. It felt shallow and empty, but his laugh relieved a little bit of the gloom that had settled about him.

"Resting in God's peace doesn't mean you aren't going to be pelted by the storms. It doesn't mean that the rain isn't going to sting any less when it hits you. But it means that you aren't going to be swallowed by it."

"It really hurts."

"Sometimes it does, Son." She went back to the pan and began serving the eggs as she continued to speak. "I remember when I was little. I used to sit on the floor while my mom would sit in her rocking chair and do her cross stitch."

Mike remembered the walls of his grandmother's home were filled embroidered birds, trees and flowers bordering the Scriptures she had painstakingly stitched over the years.

"I would look up – mind you, I could only see the bottom of it, but I would look up and wonder how she made that mess turn out to be one of those beautiful works that hung on the wall." She set his plate before him and settled into the stool next to him.

"One day, I asked her. She laughed and told me I was looking at it all from the wrong direction. The knots, the threads - they weren't the finished picture. It was the other side that had the complete picture."

Mike leaned over a little in his stool and gently nudged his mom with his shoulder. "I always did love your stories." Though he understood what she meant, he didn't see how this picture could be anything but ugly. What Russell had done to his wife was horrible. How could that not change him?

After breakfast, he hopped off the stool. "I can get some things done around the house while I'm here."

Sandra nodded her assent, but concern crinkled the corner of her smile. Mike turned from it. He didn't have an answer for the unasked questions that were swimming in her eyes.

Later that evening, Sandra sat across from him at the table. "Mike, I think every screw and bolt in this house has been sufficiently tightened."

Her statement was in response to his suggestion that tomorrow he could finish up some work his dad had started in the garage. All day long he had worked like a maniac, as if his fixing of the house could fix what was wrong with in his own home.

His mom's words echoed his thoughts. "Whatever is going on with Leanne cannot be fixed by fiddling in the garage."

"What if it can't be fixed at all?"

"Well, that is for God to decide, not you." She reached across the table and patted his hand. "I have seen God heal marriages that I thought were buried deeper than six feet under. But none of them were ever fixed without Him, and without both parties yielding to Him."

"She lied, Mom." Mike shook his head and shoved his plate away. "I'm not going to betray her trust." He scoffed at that word. Like their marriage had a shred of trust left in it – maybe it never did. "I won't dishonor her by telling you what she lied about. But she lied from day one – and now it is changing how I look at her."

"I'm not condoning her lies, but I know Leanne well enough to say she must have had, at least what she thought, was a good reason."

"I thought I knew her too, Mom." Leaning back in his chair, he shook his head. "But I don't even know anymore."

Sandra folded her napkin as she formulated her next words. Finally, she spoke. "Son, I am not sure you have ever looked at Leanne for who she really is. You see her as your ideal, and she works really hard to be that ideal for you."

At her statement, Mike sat up in anger. "I have never asked her to be anyone but who she is."

Sandra leaned back in her chair and crossed her legs. With her hands folded in her lap, she said, "I remember when you came back from your college registration. You told me about this girl you had seen there. Do you remember how you described her?"

Mike shrugged, and answered. "I said I saw this beautiful, gentle-spirited girl."

Sandra nodded. "You said she was shy, humble,

and like a beautiful flower ready to bloom."

Again Mike shrugged, not understanding his mother's point.

"You didn't even know her. You saw her from across the room, and from her smile, you gleaned all of this?"

Mike remembered her teasing him at the time about the same thing.

Sandra continued. "When you brought her home for the first time, I saw something else. I saw a beautiful flower that was trampled and crushed." Sandra tilted her head in a show of compassion and pity. "Mike, you have spent these past few years trying to make this girl bloom, but she's broken. She clung to you for support, for strength, and she drank in your love like it gave her life."

"Isn't that what I'm supposed to do?"

"Yes, to some extent." Uncrossing her legs, she leaned toward him. "Your love is not the soil she needs to be planted in. It is nice soil, but it is shallow." She tapped the table in front of him and added, "She needs richer soil and deeper roots to withstand the storms of life. You can't give her that."

Exasperation tinged his voice. "So what am I supposed to do?"

"You water her with God's truth and your love. Encourage her, but not with your infuriating inanities." She softened her tone. "A simple, *I love you*, and a kiss on the forehead aren't going to heal her. *You* are not there to make everything better for her. *You* are not there to fix her."

"Everyone keeps saying that, but..." He stopped. He knew she was right, but self-pity clouded his thoughts. *Maybe there is nothing I can do to fix her or my marriage.*

"Mike, if she's confused, you help guide her way with God's truth. If she's broken, show her how God can heal her. If she's lost in a dark place, you shine the light of God's word into her heart."

"Wash her with God's word." Mike mumbled.

Sandra nodded. "Be a reflection of God's love for her, not a substitution."

Mike stared blindly at her for a moment. Understanding hovered over him like a dark storm cloud, crashing with thunder and illuminating the sky with flashes of lighting. But the rain withheld its descent on the dry and cracked pavement of his heart.

That storm cloud stayed with him throughout the night and into the next day. With a half-hearted attitude, Mike went to work. The shop had always been a place of wonder for him as a child. His father would pick out the right tool, the right part, and fix even the most broken down car.

But as he toiled under the cars today, Mike didn't even know where to begin to fix Leanne. Russell had stripped her of her innocence, her value, her worth. How could he replace those?

*You are not there to fix her.* His mother's words plummeted from the dark cloud.

And then there was the matter of her lies. A part of him understood why she had lied, but that part was a single grain of sand on a beach that comprised one fact – she didn't trust him with the truth.

You couldn't have love without trust, so what was their marriage built on?

*Your love is not the soil she needs to be planted in.* Like heavy raindrops, Sandra's statement fell into his heart.

Guilt came washing over him at the track of his thoughts. He tried to understand where she was coming from. He chuckled to himself as he thought of all the times she had proven over the years that you need to look deeper than the person's actions. She had lied, but deeper than that was her pain, her twisted sense of self and shaky faith. Now she was trying to make it better; she was trying to make it right. And he was underneath this car condemning her for her brave step forward.

*You see her as your ideal, and she works really hard to be that ideal for you.*

He put the tool down next to him, and closed his eyes. He knew what he needed to do.

Staying at his mom's was just delaying the inevitable. He'd return home and let her know his decision.

## Chapter Fourteen

Leanne closed the nearly empty dishwasher and turned it on. There weren't many dishes with just her and the kids. The room was immaculate. After putting the kids to bed, she had scrubbed the counters until they shined.

She sniffled back her tears. If it weren't for Windex and the Bible, Leanne would have gone mad these past two days. She had alternated between cleaning and praying over God's word. She cleaned as if scrubbing every inch of the house could make amends for the mess she had made of their marriage. Then, when she was exhausted from her efforts, she would fall on her knees and cry into her open Bible. She grabbed verses as if they were life-lines, keeping her afloat as the water swirled around her and the storm threatened to swallow her whole.

The more she prayed and flipped through the pages in His word, the calmer the storm felt, and she was able to stand again.

But as she moved about the house, a house that Mike had yet to return to, the storm would pick up in strength again.

Karen had been upset at her dad's absence. When the little girl asked, a lie sprang to Leanne's lips to shelter the little girl from the truth. *No more lies.* Instead, Leanne had said, "Daddy just needs to spend some time at Grandma's. His heart is sad."

But even her attempt at being right seemed to

mock her, taunting her with more pain. As she was tucking Karen into bed tonight, the little girl said, "Mommy, you should go to Grandma's too."

A sad attempt at a laugh escaped, sounding more like an amused sigh. "Why, sweetie?"

"Because your heart is sad, too."

The stinging truth of her daughter's words still hung about her as she wiped a nonexistent speck from the counter.

Nothing left to do but to crawl into bed...alone.

Heading toward their bedroom, she stopped at the sound of keys in the lock.

*Mike!* She inhaled deeply, steeling herself for the worst, but praying for the best.

Mike placed his suitcase down on the entryway floor as she came to stand a couple feet from him.

She stared at him, her chin quivering and his nostrils fluttering from suppressed tears. Neither moved; neither crossed the distance that separated them. Leanne knew she couldn't take the steps that would bring her into the one place she wanted to be – his arms.

She had no right. She had to leave it up to him, and from his stony silence, she feared the worst.

It seemed like an eternity stretched before he finally spoke. "Leanne, I want you to know I am not mad at you."

He ran a hand through his hair, closing his eyes as if he couldn't look at her. "I am mad that you didn't tell me all these years."

The pain, the hurt she saw in his steel gray eyes

felt like a million bees stinging her heart.

"I understand the trust issues you might..." He shook his head and closed the distance between them. His carefully restrained emotion broke through, and his words washed over her in a rush. "No, I don't understand. I could have helped you through it." Gripping her arms lightly, he scanned her features as if he might find the answer there.

Leanne wanted to say she was sorry, or offer up an explanation, but she just stood there.

He let go of her arms as if her skin burned his hands, and he turned his body away from her, refusing to touch her or look at her. "I need you to understand that I do not blame you for what happened with Russell. This is not what this is about."

Leanne braced for the hammer to fall. *Just say it!* She wanted to scream. *End it now so I can start picking up the pieces.*

Mike turned back to her, cradling her face in his large hands, her hair creating a blonde curtain over them. He placed his forehead against hers and breathed deeply. "I love you."

His words broke the bonds that held her silent. She placed her hands on his forearms. "Mike, I love you, too. Please don't go."

His thumbs caressed her cheeks, his eyes scanned her features, and his lips began their descent toward hers. But they stopped shy of their mark, and nothing could have been more brutal to Leanne's battered heart at that moment. While she knew that his cruel actions were not intentional, that didn't stop the pain from searing her heart.

He released her face, stepping back from her as he said, "I'm not leaving, but I can't just pick up as if nothing happened."

Her eyes filled with tears as she nodded her head as if she understood. From the look on his face, though, she really didn't think time was going to make any difference. She had hurt him, lied to him, and she didn't know how they could come back from that.

Leanne finally found the courage to ask, "Are you going back to your mom's?"

Mike shook his head, eliciting a sigh of relief from her. But her relief was short-lived. "I don't want to be separated from the kids. And Karen's evaluation...I should be here for that."

*Of course*, she thought, *the kids.*

She headed back to their room and gathered up her nightgown. When she made for the guest room, he stopped her. "Where are you going?"

Confusion knit her brow. She had assumed he wouldn't want her near him. "The guest room...I thought..."

His words came out harsh, and she couldn't tell if it was from anger or regret. "No, you belong here with me."

Though his tone held little forgiveness, his words buoyed her hope, but only briefly. "Sleeping in another room, me staying with my mom...that's not right."

Leanne nodded in submission and numbly walked

to the bathroom to change. When she slipped under the cover moments later, his back was turned. The rift between them in the bed widened as anger mounted slowly within her heart. *Perfect Mike, always the one to do things right! And if it isn't right, he's got to fix it right away.* She quietly dashed her tears from her cheeks, but as she closed her eyes, more tears escaped. *Your picture-perfect, unspoiled life leaves little room for me, Mike McKinley.*

---

"Karen does not have autism." Mike whispered in her ear as they sat in the psychiatrist's office. She followed his eyes to a little boy whose mom was trying to talk to him. Instead, he was fascinated by the rotation of the blades on the ceiling fan. The boy hadn't spoken during the entire hour they had been in the waiting room.

Dr. Meston had referred them to a clinic in Albuquerque that dealt only with autism spectrum disorders. After their arrival at the clinic, Dr. Mark Siglia, a tall thin man with turquoise rectangular framed glasses, had greeted them and said he wanted to meet with Karen first, before he spoke with them. They watched as the doctor and a woman ushered Karen back to the office while Mike and Leanne filled out a stack of questionnaires.

Fifteen minutes after Karen was gone, Dr. Siglia returned for them. When they entered his office, Karen was in an adjacent room, and Mike and Leanne could see her playing behind a glass window with the same woman who had led her away.

"Thank you for letting me speak with her first." Dr. Siglia said while he closed the door and took a seat across from them. "It helps me get a sense of who she is before I hear it from you."

They nodded, not knowing what else to say.

"I can see you have been given our legendary stack of forms." His smile was warm and inviting, like a crackling fire on a cold winter's night. Leanne felt herself relaxing a bit in his presence.

"These questionnaires, along with the tests we are going to do tomorrow, will give us an idea of how she functions, how her brain works, sensory issues, and the like."

"Sensory issues?" Mike and Leanne asked in unison.

"Do lights bother her, sounds, background noises, texture of food, clothing..."

His voice trailed off as they looked at each other. "Her buttons."

Mike chimed in behind her. "Loud noises, and even the constant background noise of something bothers her."

Leanne nodded. "The window air conditioner in your dad's office."

The doctor nodded while jotting noted down in his yellow legal pad. "How about emotions? How does she express emotions?"

Mike and Leanne glanced at each other before Mike shrugged. "I think she expresses emotions well." He gazed down at Leanne with a smile, the first genuine one they'd shared in weeks. "In her own way. Remember that time she started screaming that line from Veggie Tales?"

Leanne laughed, and turned to Dr. Siglia. "She took the emotion from the scene, but used the words – even though they didn't fit what was happening."

"Give me an example?"

"Once she was angry at me for something..."

When Mike looked to her for guidance, she shook her head. "I can't remember what it was."

"...she screamed at me, 'I'm sixteen years old, I can do what I want!' She loved the Little Mermaid, and we immediately recognized that line from the movie."

Dr. Siglia nodded his head, smiling. "It is like echolalia, but with her emotions."

Leanne remembered that Mrs. Henley had said Karen used echolalia in communicating. From the glance she exchanged with Mike, she knew he was recalling that as well.

As the session wore on, Leanne's heart grew heavy. The more Dr. Siglia explained autism, the more she realized that her daughter fit into these descriptions.

Mike, on the other hand, only grew more frustrated as the session continued. Her heart went out to him, because she knew that her daughter had just landed into the same category as she did – something that couldn't be fixed.

"What I find interesting is that she is so young, and she clearly has deficits in communication and social skills, yet she has found her own way of crossing these deficits."

Mike and Leanne looked at each other, not knowing how to feel about the doctor's statement.

Dr. Siglia smiled, reading the confusion on their faces. "That is actually a good thing."

Leanne was still holding onto that glimmer of hope the doctor had offered to them as Mike and Leanne sat on the bed in the hotel room that evening. They had been given more forms before leaving, and the stacks sat between them as they worked to complete them.

She jumped when Mike threw his pen down and sighed in exasperation. "These questions are ridiculous. 'Does your child pretend to play with toys such as feeding dolls, or putting stuffed animals to sleep?' I think I've answered that question three times already."

He looked up at her finally, and she saw the glimmer of tears in his eyes. She reached across and placed her hand on his. It was the first time they had purposely touched since the night he came home.

"Whatever happens, whatever diagnosis they give her, she is still going to be Karen." For Leanne, the role of comforter was like a cumbersome snowsuit, awkward to wear, but serving its purpose.

He stared at her for a moment, a variety of emotions playing across his handsome features. For a second, Leanne thought he might bridge the distance between them, but, in the end, Mike slipped his hand out from under hers to swipe it down his face in frustration. "I know, but I read that pamphlet in the office. It said she would have it for life. It's not like she's going to grow out of it, or we can fix it..."

Anger boiled up within Leanne - anger that had been suppressed for years. She tried to cap it, but it would not be contained.

"Not everything needs fixing!" Leanne bit out between clenched teeth.

Mike leaned back at the ferocity of her tone. She softened her next words, but only because she didn't want to wake Karen, who as sleeping on the bed next to theirs.

"She might not be perfect, but she's pretty amazing. I heard what he said about sensory issues and the anxiety change causes her." She gathered up her half of the forms from the bed. "I read between the lines. I can see how scary the world probably is to her."

Scrambling off the bed, she turned back toward him, the forms clutched tightly to her chest as if she was trying to contain the roiling emotions within it. Her lips trembled as she spoke up for her daughter and for herself. "Despite that, she has found a way to make it through. It might not be the way you do things, and maybe she makes mistakes, but she's doing her best. So stop trying to fix her and just love her for who she is."

She stormed out of the room and went down to the hotel lobby. Getting a cup of coffee, she sat down at one of the couches in front of a large TV with the news playing. But she was oblivious to all that was around her. Her chest was still heaving from the anger within her.

She struggled to focus on the forms. Tears and defeat had been a refrain playing over and over in her life, but her momentary explosion felt good. She wasn't hiding behind what everyone else wanted of her, expected of her, or believed she was. Leanne McKinley was a broken woman, with a past so horrific, it would make you want to gag on your breakfast. But she had come to a crossroads the night before her stepfather's funeral in a hotel just shy of Albuquerque, New Mexico. She could have continued to settle for her broken identity. She could have endured walking around in defeat, struggling with her sins. Instead, she had fallen to her knees and sought healing from God.

No, she hadn't sought healing; she had pursued God with an unwavering resolve. With grit that she didn't believe she possessed, she swore not to get off her knees, not to cease her prayers, until she had found peace that night.

Leanne lifted her chin a little, feeling freedom's cool breeze through her spirit, calming the hot anger. *I was broken, but God is rebuilding me.*

As hard as it was to come home and tell Mike the truth, she had a greater aversion to giving up the precious peace that invaded her life, and she knew that meant not allowing her lies, her pain and her past to infect their marriage anymore. She wanted to rebuild their marriage, but it had to be on solid ground.

*What a blessing to find a man so blind to your faults.* Her mom's words at their wedding slithered into her mind. Now that his eyes were open, it appeared like he didn't like what he saw.

She closed her eyes at the thought. Dashing a tear that had escaped, she turned her attention to the forms. *Please don't let that be true, God.*

## Chapter Fifteen

Mike's hand rested on his thigh, a few inches from Leanne's. A second in time, a scant distance, a single movement would close the space between them. She could imagine the sweet feeling of his warm hand wrapped around hers.

She tried to focus her attention back to Nathan as he spoke from the pulpit.

Over the years, there had been countless times the two of them had held hands during worship, through the sermon, or in prayer. A simple action she had disregarded before, but an intimacy that Leanne longed for now.

To Leanne, it was physical representation of becoming one, standing together, agreeing that God was sovereign in their lives, their hearts and their marriage.

A month had passed since Karen's evaluation. When she had stormed out of that hotel room, something had changed for her. She wasn't willing to settle for the way things were before. She wanted to know Mike loved her for who she really was - broken but being beautifully repaired by God.

Instead, Mike walked around like a ghost of his former self. He was pensive and brooding, and the rift between them grew slowly and silently. He was kind to her - Mike was always perfectly kind - but his politeness felt like sandpaper, and his touch always fell short of its mark. Which is why Leanne knew it was pointless to reach for his hand now.

She stole a glance at him and found he wasn't listening to Nathan either. Following his gaze, she saw he was staring at a woman sitting across the church. She felt the chasm widen and she grabbed for his hand, afraid they'd both fall through.

His startled gaze fell on her, and she stared up at him, silently begging him to come back to her.

But all she saw in his steely gray eyes was confusion. His grip was loose, not reciprocating. A flicker of emotion followed by a momentary squeeze gave her hope. But he slid his hand out from hers, placing it along the back of the pew.

*Not around my shoulders, but on the pew, so he doesn't have to touch me, and I can't touch him.*

She hung her head, her blond hair creating a veil to hide her tears. She had quietly given him space and time, but he had just grown more distant. Her chin quivered. She couldn't spend the rest of her life settling for his polite indifference. Their marriage was in a coma – and her love was the living breathing mind trapped in an unmoving body.

*Help me fight for us, God.*

She surreptitiously brushed the tears from her face, enduring Mike's distant but close proximity, and turned her head toward Nathan. She half listened to his sermon on Hosea.

After service, Kristina pulled her to the side.

"Are you ready to go next weekend?"

With their marriage in the midst of a storm, the last thing Leanne had wanted to do was go on a weekend spa retreat with the rest of Kristina's bridal party. But after this morning, she felt that a little distance between them would help her sort out what she needed to do next.

Leanne nodded and forced a smile. Kristina and Kristina might not be close friends, but, over the past year, they had formed an inexplicable bond – a nameless kinship that went beyond just their future in-law status. It was from that bond that Kristina asked, "Are you nervous about Karen, or is it Mike?"

The tension Leanne had been holding in her shoulders relaxed a bit. "Is it that obvious?"

"No, but I know a woman who is holding a weight on her shoulders when I see one."

Leanne's eyes searched for Mike in the congregation as she responded. "I spent the first years of our marriage with a clouded spiritual life, but what I thought was a strong marriage." She shrugged, defeat creeping into her tone. "Now that I finally feel like I have God's peace in my heart, I see our marriage slipping away."

"I know things might look bad, but they always do in the midst of a storm. You are going to doubt a lot of things right now. Mike loves you." Kristina hugged her, and added, "Don't ever doubt that."

Leanne returned the embrace, finally catching sight of Mike over Kristina's shoulder. He was talking to the woman who he had been staring at during service. The woman leaned close to him as she spoke, placing her hand along his bicep.

"Who is that woman?" Leanne asked Nathan, who had just joined them.

Nathan followed Leanne's gaze. "Oh, that is Laura. She's the sister of my high school friend."

"They look pretty chummy." Leanne mumbled as she watched Mike's face light up in a smile at something the beautiful red-haired woman said. She was nearly as tall as Mike, lithe and willowy. Her long golden red-hair shone like a halo about her and fell down well past her shoulders. She was gorgeous, confident, and perfect.

"They briefly dated right before he left for college." Nathan nudged Leanne. "That's not jealousy I hear, is it?"

Leanne looked at him, and the sadness in her eyes must have touched a nerve in his heart, because all teasing was erased from his face. "Leanne, Mike loves you. He'd never be unfaithful."

She nodded, wanting to believe his words.

Nathan continued, hoping to put her fears to rest, but his words brought little comfort. If anything, they solidified her fears. "Mike and Laura were already split up when he went to college registration. But when he saw you, he came home and couldn't talk about anyone else. As hard as Laura pursued him, he pursued you three times as hard."

But that was the Leanne he wanted to see, the Leanne she had allowed him to see. He had pursued a lie. Leanne tried to argue with her thoughts, but a glance across the room at the smiling couple strengthened her fears.

Mike turned toward her, and their eyes met across the room. She saw that same flicker of emotion she had seen during the service.

*Now that he can see the real me, I am sure he's wishing he'd stayed with Laura.*

That train of thought didn't dissipate on the silent ride home.

It stayed with her all week, as each day fell with despair from the calendar page. She had wanted to rebuild their marriage on truth, but all she had done was start building a wall between them.

The only relief to their separation came on Wednesday, when they traveled up to get the results of Karen's evaluation. As Dr. Siglia explained the tests, the scores, what they meant, and where Karen fell on the spectrum, Leanne couldn't stop the tears from falling.

Dr. Siglia handed her a box of tissues, and she accepted it. But what she longed for was the strength of the man next to her. She wanted to feel his arm around her shoulders, she wanted to hear his "It will be okay," and she wanted to have their fingers intertwined. She wanted to know that they were one and she wasn't going to have to do this on her own.

Instead, she sat suffering in silence, listening to the doctor explain what came next, while the litany of guilty self-accusations paraded around her head. They tormented her throughout the visit, until she couldn't stand it anymore. When they all stood to exit, Leanne sat back down.

Her blue eyes were pooling with tears and large in her stricken face. "What causes...I mean, did I do something..."

Mike sat next to her, grabbing her hand for the first time. "Leanne, don't even think that."

While the doctor assured her she wasn't the cause of her daughter's diagnosis, she drew strength more from her husband's hand, his gentle assurances, and the look in his eyes.

She wanted desperately to hang on to him, but they had to leave. As they rose to exit the office, he let go of her hand.

*Please, God. I saw that look in his eyes. It wasn't just pity; it wasn't just compassion. It was that loving look he used to give me.*

Later at the hotel, as they got ready to go to sleep, Mike stopped her. Taking her by the hand, he turned her to look at him. "I don't want you to think that this is your fault."

The emotional day had taken its toll on her. She didn't know if he was referring to Karen's diagnosis or their situation, but she charged ahead anyway. She had been keeping all her emotions bottled up for years, and his words pried the cork off the bottle.

"When I was eighteen, sitting on that cold hospital bed in the ER, my stepfather - the father of my miscarried baby - standing next to me, I felt both relief and sadness." Though she had longed for closeness, she removed her hand from his and crossed her arms in front of her chest. "When I found out I was pregnant, I kept it a secret. I was just going to run away and be free." Leanne's chin quivered, and she struggled to suppress her tears. "I just wanted to be free, and I kept praying for it all to just go away. And then I miscarried..."

Mike tucked her wayward strand behind her ear. The familiar gesture cut through her heart, but she continued. "Now, I can't help wondering if everything isn't consequences for my sins."

Mike took her gently by the arms. "What Russell did to you is his sin, not yours."

"Maybe, but it feels like I am the one paying for those sins." She looked up at him, a tear escaping as she gently touched his cheek. "And those around me have paid dearly, too."

Mike closed his eyes at her touch.

Stepping out of his arms, she trudged forward with what she had been praying about all week. "Mike, I know I hurt you with my lies. I don't think I could ever apologize enough for that."

"I know you are sorry, Leanne. And I don't want you to ever think that I'm angry about your past." He stepped forward and brushed his thumb across her cheek. "My distance isn't about punishing you for your past, or even the lies I think you told because you felt you didn't have a choice. I understand that."

Confusion knit her brow. She had assumed all along that he was upset with her for the lies.

"It is just..." Mike cupped her face between his large calloused palms, rough from years of fixing things that were broken. His eyes searched her face as if he could find the answers to his jumbled emotions on hers.

Leanne grabbed his wrists and slowly pulled his hands from her face. "It's just you don't know how to fix this. You don't know how to erase my past, or put the pieces of my broken life back together."

A teary smile filled her face as she took a step back, spreading her arms wide. "This is me, Mike. I'm broken, scarred and imperfect. There is nothing you can do or say that is going to change that." Putting her arms down in defeat, she added. "You just need to figure out if you can love me like this."

# Chapter Sixteen

Mike stared blindly at the stack of invoices on his desk, his mind on the image of Leanne packing her suitcase this morning.

He shoved the stack to the side, burying his head in his hands. Her words in the hotel room haunted him all week. His first reaction had been to reject her theory that he was stalling because he couldn't fix her and that he wasn't able to love her for who she was. But his mom's comments also came back, and the two women's words played a twisted game of Ring-Around-the-Rosie in his brain all yesterday.

Of course he loved her for who she was; she was *his* Leanne.

But then why was he delaying? Why wasn't he comforting her? He had heard the pain she was going through, the pain she had been through. Her tale of the night she had miscarried had torn at his heart.

*...my stepfather, the father of my miscarried baby, standing next to me, I felt both relief and sadness...*

He pictured that eighteen year old Leanne, struggling under the burden of her dark secret, a mother who showed her no love all her life, confused and alone. Who did she have to turn to? And when she had unburdened herself to him, when she finally sought freedom in the truth, he had shackled her again with guilt.

Instead of holding her, he distanced himself from her. Instead of helping her, he hurt her. Instead of love, he chose to dwell in anger.

*But, God, I wasn't angry at her.* Mike prayed silently. *I was angry at Russell, and angry at myself. All these years I have failed her. My mom is right, I have always seen her as I wanted to see her. I never saw her pain and I let her suffer.*

He thought about how she had reached for his hand in church. It had felt so good, but he had let go. He felt guilty touching her.

*I don't want to hurt her. What if, when I touch her, she is reminded of Russell?*

Though he tried to shake the thought from his mind, it had been plaguing him for weeks now. Scenes from their marriage had been playing in his mind and he analyzed each one. What did he miss? Where had he shown her he couldn't be trusted? When had he shown her he didn't love her? But the look on her face as she asked him if he could love her for who she was called all his past actions into question.

The verses from Sunday's sermon paraded through his head. They had been all week. Though the second chapter of Hosea describes God's love for unfaithful Israel, he couldn't shake the picture it painted of his wife's journey back to God. Verses 14 through 16 said

> "But then I will win her back once again.
>    I will lead her into the desert
>    and speak tenderly to her there.
> I will return her vineyards to her

and transform the Valley of Trouble into a gateway of hope.
She will give herself to me there,
> as she did long ago when she was young,
> when I freed her from her captivity in Egypt.

When that day comes," says the Lord,
> "you will call me 'my husband'
> instead of 'my master.'"

It was the difference between husband and master that had really stuck with him. Those three verses detailed his wife's transformation spiritually. She had told him the truth, not out of simple obedience to God, but because she loved Him. She had chosen God, not as a simple matter of authority, but a choice born of love. A love that was possible because God had first pursued her with love, and she had chosen to reach out for Him.

He opened the Bible app on his phone and pulled up verses 19 through 21.

I will make you my wife forever,
> showing you righteousness and justice,
> unfailing love and compassion.

I will be faithful to you and make you mine,
> and you will finally know me as the Lord.

"In that day, I will answer,"
> says the Lord.

"I will answer the sky as it pleads for clouds.
And the sky will answer the earth with rain.

He stared at his phone for a moment, rereading those verses until he leaned back in his chair.

The more he read those verses, the more he felt as if God was telling him, "I called her back to Me and she came. I turned her valley of trouble into hope, and she surrendered herself to that hope, regardless of the consequences she might have faced from you. I've established with her a covenant based on My righteousness, mercy, grace and love. Your love for her should be a reflection of that covenant."

A month ago, his mom had told him to be an echo of God's love, not a substitution. Leanne was like a barren desert, eager for rain, and he had spent all those years keeping her from God's downpour by making it all about what he could do for her, instead of what God could do within her.

Jumping up from his desk, he grabbed his keys and stormed to his truck.

On the short drive to his house, he kept repeating his silent apologies to God. He knew he had been on the wrong side of compassion, grace and mercy. Now, he vowed to show her he was wrong, how sorry he was, and beg for her forgiveness.

Pulling up in the driveway, he had barely taken the keys out of the ignition when he jumped out of the truck. When he ran inside the house, he found it was empty. She must have left early for the bridal party trip.

It only took him a second before he stormed back out to his truck and headed for his mom's. He knew she had to drop the kids off with Sandra; maybe he hadn't missed her yet. But as he turned down his parent's street, he could see that her car wasn't in the driveway.

His foot eased off the accelerator and he let his truck drift into the driveway. Earlier, his steps held an urgency, now his feet dragged under the weight of the realization that he would have to wait until Sunday evening to speak with her.

When his mom opened the door, he tried to muster some joy. "Hey, Mom."

"I hope you don't think you are going to whisk my grandkids away from me when Leanne just dropped them off."

Mike walked past her and sank down in the sofa, shaking his head no. "I was hoping to catch her."

His mom crossed her arms over her chest and asked, "You finally came to your senses?"

Mike tried to laugh, but a sob got tangled up in it. "I've been so foolish, focused on what I *could* do, or what I *shouldn't* do. Mom, I must have caused her so much pain, and after all she's been through…"

Sandra sat down next to her son and placed her hand atop his. "Mike, she broke down in tears and told me what happened before she left."

Mike jerked his head up at his mom's statement. Guilt opened a wider cut in his heart as he realized why Leanne had confided in his mom. He had left her with no choice; he had left her alone to worry and wonder. "Oh, Mom, I really messed things up."

"Yes, you did." Sandra laughed, ruffling his hair like she did when he was a kid. "Are you ready to start yielding to God and letting Him fix things?"

"What if she doesn't...?"

His mom cut off his words. "Trust me, she has surrendered your marriage to God."

"But I was so angry at her for not trusting me."

"Since that man started to violate her, she began to mistrust everything around her, including herself. How was she going to trust you when she didn't even trust God?"

Mike shrugged his shoulders, and his mom continued. "And given her past, I think she trusted you in her own way."

"But..."

"I saw the way she looked at you, clung to you, and sought out your love. It might not have been healthy for her, but you were the solid ground she stood on."

"And when she needed me most, I crumbled right underneath her feet, letting her fall."

"Mike McKinley, do you think she could have told you the truth without trusting God? She kept that secret for eight years, she could have kept it for eight more without you ever knowing. It was when she yielded to God, when she surrendered to Him, that she began to let go of everything. She stopped leaning on you, and started to lean on Him."

Mike thought back to how she looked in the hotel room. Though she was hurting, she had strength. Though she was crying, she had peace. And even in the midst of the storm, she stood solidly.

"With courage, she told me the truth because it is

what God asked her to do. And she's been patiently waiting for me to begin rebuilding our marriage."

"So what are you going to do about it?" His mom asked.

"I'm going to be the husband God has called me to be."

---

The next morning, Mike sipped his third cup of coffee as he fixed the kids their breakfast. Last night he had slept little, and he was looking forward to the day with the kids to keep his mind off of Leanne.

The doorbell rang, and Mike opened the door to find his mom on the doorstep. She kissed him on the cheek and then brushed past him. "Good morning, Son. Where are my grandbabies?"

"Eating breakfast. What are you doing here so early?" Mike ran a hand across his still stubbly chin.

"Coming to take them from you."

"You're stealing my kids?"

Sandra gave her son a look that clearly said she didn't appreciate his sarcasm. "Grandmothers do not steal." Placing her purse on the counter, she kissed each of the kids on the tops of their heads. "I think you need some more quiet time."

"Mom, I wanted to spend the day with the kids, not sit alone in this empty house." Mike protested. The last thing he wanted to do was wander aimlessly with his own tormented thoughts. He hadn't slept all last night. He was anxious for Leanne's return, but nervous that she would turn her back on him. He had treated her so badly…

"Then don't. Go to the garage and tinker with the cars. That always helps you clear your head."

"I don't tinker, Mom."

Sandra waved away his objections. "Don't argue with your mother. You are setting a bad example in front of your kids."

Mike chuckled. "That was a low blow, Mom."

Sandra's smile showed she might agree, but she didn't care.

An hour later, Mike found himself underneath a car, doing exactly what his mom said, trying to clear his head. Leanne would be home tomorrow. The thought sent glee and fear skittering across his heart.

"Hello?" Mike emerged from underneath the car at the sound of a female voice.

"Laura?" Mike asked, wiping his hands on a rag. "What are you doing here?"

"I heard you were here all alone. I thought I'd come by and see if you want to have lunch, you know, catch up on old times." The woman was wearing a dress that clung to every curve of her body, and the way she was looking at him made him wished he'd stayed under the car.

"I'm good, I've got a sandwich in the office for later…" Mike's voice trailed off as he fought to keep his eyes averted from her.

"Well, let me go grab something and we can eat together."

"Laura, I don't think that would be a good idea."

She sidled up to him and took the towel from his

hands, wiping a smudge of grease from his cheeks. "Maybe not, but I hear that your marriage isn't doing so well."

Mike took the towel from her hands. "Laura, I love my wife."

"I hear you two are as close as California and Alabama. You spend time away from her." She edged a little closer to him. "I know you thought she was so perfect. After you saw her, I didn't have a chance of reuniting with you." She placed her hands along his forearms and pouted in a sultry fashion meant to entice him. "Now that your little snow white is all muddy, maybe I have a chance."

Whatever Laura had hoped to accomplish, her words caused guilt to dig its nails deeper into his heart. He had hurt Leanne so much over the years…

Mike's tortured thoughts were interrupted as Laura Leaned in for a kiss. He was barely able to step away from her before her lips landed on his.

"Laura!" Mike roared. "I don't know what you've heard, but I love my wife. There isn't any way this" he pointed back and forth between them, "is happening." Mike took the towel and wiped the wet spot where her lips had grazed. "Please leave."

Laura pouted, and then shrugged. "Suit yourself. But the offer still stands if you change your mind. I think you know where to find me."

He stood staring out the bay doors long after she had walked through them. Throwing the rag down, he ran a hand down his face in frustration.

Laura had said that she'd heard their marriage

wasn't doing well. Mike closed his eyes and thought, *just another way I've hurt and dishonored her. God, please let her forgive me. I know I haven't done much lately to warrant her mercy, but I beg you to soften her heart toward me.*

# Chapter Seventeen

Up at the Triple R Resort, Leanne was having a hard time trying to relax and enjoy the weekend. Her mind kept wandering back to her marriage. She didn't regret telling Mike the truth, she was just sad things hadn't turned out like she wanted them to. Their marriage had become a cold, silent dance between two strangers, and though she didn't want their marriage to end, she couldn't continue on in the way they had been.

*I love you, God. I did what You asked. That really is enough for me; Your love is enough. Regardless, I will rest in you, Lord.*

That was her mantra – if she kept saying it enough, she hoped the pain would eventually ease.

"Can I do your hair for tonight's dinner?" Barbara's voice pulled Leanne out of her thoughts. She was sharing a suite with Barbara, while Kristina and Lisa, Kristina's best friend and matron of honor, were in the room next to theirs.

Leanne shrugged, allowing the girl to push her gently down in a chair in front of the mirror. Barbara had been attacked a couple of weeks before her high school graduation, and Leanne had been impressed with her courage when she had fought the wealth and power of the Swanson family to make sure their son was punished for what he did. At the same time, Leanne felt guilty when she learned that the girl was pregnant and had decided to keep the baby instead of putting it up for adoption. Barbara was the same age that Leanne was when she found out she was pregnant with Russell's child.

*She fought - you gave up.*

Catching Leanne's look, Barbara asked, "What?"

"I was just thinking how brave you have been." Leanne saw a shadow pass over the young girl's face, and Leanne was immediately sorry for speaking up. "I'm sorry, I shouldn't have pried."

Barbara shook her head. "No, it's okay. I don't know if I would call myself brave. Sometimes I feel like I am just getting by each day, fighting with all my emotions, fighting just to take my next breath."

Leanne nodded; she understood all too well what the young girl was talking about. There were days where she felt like she was standing firmly on the shore, the water merely kissing her heels. There were other days where she felt as if she were being sucked down a river, struggling to break free from the water's grasp.

"But I have Amari, so giving up is not an option."

"She is a beautiful little girl."

The smile returned to the young woman's face. "She is what I fight for."

Leanne thought about this throughout dinner, where she distractedly joined in the conversation. As they were heading up to their rooms for the night, Kristina pulled her to the side.

Leanne felt bad. This was her soon to be sister-in-law's bridal weekend, and she was self-absorbed in her own problems. Before the woman could say anything to Leanne, she apologized. "Kristina, I am sorry if I have been so downcast ..."

Kristina cut her off. "Leanne, I am the one who is sorry. I know you and Mike have a lot going on right now, and if you want to go home, I won't be offended."

"No, I want to stay. Besides, I still need to sort some things out and make a decision about what I'm going to do when I get home."

Kristina nodded slowly, but then paused and shook her head. "When Nathan and I broke up last year, I thought that I had done too much to hurt him. My past was like this great army that I had let it trample over everything good in my life.

Leanne knew they had broken up right around the time Barbara had been attacked, but she didn't know why they had separated.

Kristina continued. "I have learned that circumstances happen, life changes in the blink of an eye, our hearts and emotions will deceive us, and that people will more than likely let you down."

*Wow, don't sugar coat it, Kristina,* Leanne thought.

Taking her firmly by the shoulders, Kristina continued. "We need to plant our self in the truth that comes only from God's word, let our roots reach down deep into the hope, joy and peace that only He can provide, and draw strength from the Holy Spirit."

Leanne nodded, hanging her head to hide her tears. "I know, trust in His plan. And I do..."

"But that doesn't mean you can't fight, Leanne,"

Kristina interrupted. "As long as you are fighting for what God wants you to fight for, you do it humbly from your knees first, and you recognize that He is really the one doing the fighting."

The two women walked to their rooms in silence, but at their doors, Kristina said, "In the first chapter of Joshua, God tells him to be strong and courageous over and over. He didn't say, 'don't be afraid, Joshua, I made you a really strong warrior,' or 'I made you a military strategy genius.' God told Joshua repeatedly not to fear because God was going to be with him."

Kristina wrapped Leanne in a hug and said, "Go fight for your marriage. Be strong and courageous because God is with you."

"I will."

There wasn't much enthusiasm in her voice. As a result, Kristina firmly grasped Leanne's shoulders and said, "Leanne, you have surrendered your life to Christ, so don't let the enemy come in and recapture ground that doesn't belong to him. Your marriage belongs to God. Stand firm, and don't let the enemy put so much as his pinkie toe in it."

Leanne laughed, and this time there was more conviction behind her statement. "I will."

Saturday morning, when dawn streaked across the sky, Leanne rose and began packing.

"What's going on?" Came Barbara's sleepy question. "Has something happened?"

"No," Leanne looked up and laughed. "Yes, I have decided to fight."

Exhilaration lent a little bit of a hysterical tone to Leanne's voice, causing a look of concern from Barbara. "How late did you stay up reading the Bible?"

Leanne zipped up her suitcase and plunked her hands on her hips in a satisfied manner. "Long enough to know what I should be doing."

"Which is..."

"I told you, fighting." Leanne sat on the bed to slip on her shoes. "I have let storms ravage my life one too many times. Afterwards, I pick up the pieces, having lost one or two in the storm, and do my best to move on." With her shoes on, Leanne stood and looked Barbara firmly in the eye.

Barbara rubbed the sleep from her eyes and said slowly. "Okay..."

"Barbara, I have let the enemy surround me, and I have let him have ground in my marriage that he should have never had. Today is the day to stand firm. Today is the day I stop settling and start fighting."

Leanne left a sleepy and confused Barbara as she headed to tell Kristina she was heading home.

Two hours later, when she finally reached Hamilton, she found the house empty. She dialed Mike's number, but only got his voicemail.

"How wonderful that you came home early!" Sandra exclaimed when Leanne called her a few moments later. "But no, Mike's not here. I took the kids for the day. He probably went to the shop."

Leanne's heart skipped a few beats on the drive to

the garage, as doubts ran through her mind. She thought of all his cool indifference lately. What if he didn't want her anymore?

She tried to shake the doubts from her mind, reminding herself that she was there to fight. Pulling up in the garage, she headed toward the open bay door, but came up short at the sound of a woman's voice.

"I hear you two are as close as California and Alabama. You spend time away from her. I know you *thought* she was so perfect. After you saw her, I didn't have a chance of reuniting with you." Leanne didn't need to see the woman to know that was Laura, Mike's old girlfriend.

Leanne covered her mouth to hold back the sob when she heard the woman say, "Now that your little snow white is all muddy, maybe I have a chance."

Running back to her car, she pulled out of the parking lot and headed back toward their house.

*No, God!*

She hadn't gone a block before she pulled into a gas station and allowed her tears to fall unheeded. Leaning her head back against the headrest, she closed her eyes.

*He can't forgive me, and he's moved on. No wonder he's been so distant...*

She tried to reconcile her out-of-control train of thought with the man she knew. Mike was a man of integrity.

Kristina's words trickled through her mind. *Your marriage belongs to God. Stand firm, and don't let the enemy put so much as his pinkie toe in it.*

Leanne dashed her tears and turned her car around to head back to the garage. Once she got there, she slammed the car door loud enough to announce her presence, and marched straight into the bay. The fear of seeing Mike in another woman's arms caused her feet to falter a bit in their determined march toward reclaiming her marriage.

She breathed an inward sigh of relief when she saw Mike was alone and was locking up his office. *Was he locking up to meet Laura?*

He came up short when he saw her, his eyes taking in her cheeks stained with tears.

"Leanne." Her name was like a precious whisper across his lips. He made a step toward her, but she backed up.

"Leanne, you are home early. What happened?"

"Mike, I came back early to fight for our marriage."

He took a step towards her at her words, but she halted his step with her next sentence. "I saw you with Laura."

His face blanched, and she prayed that it wasn't a sign of guilt.

"Leanne..."

She interrupted him. "I came back to fight for our marriage and you are throwing it away on that girl."

Mike opened his mouth to protest, but she stopped him. "I don't know where you are in this marriage, but I want to rebuild it - if it's not too late." The last sentence came out in a whisper, and she searched his steel gray eyes, looking for a clue as to how he felt.

"I promise you, I didn't...I wouldn't." Mike raked a hand down his face in frustration. "I sent her away with a clear understanding that I was not interested. Nothing happened..." He closed the distance between them. "I would never do anything to hurt you..."

His words trailed off at her incredulous expression.

"But you have. In your effort to fix me, you hurt me. You are not God. You can't do what only Jesus can do – save me, heal me, and make me clean. I have to walk through this with Him. What I needed was your support. You rejected me."

From the look on his face, her words must have stung. "I am sorry." His words were a humble whisper.

"I want our marriage back, but not the way it was. I want you to love me where I am right now, but encourage me to be all that God created me to be."

Unable to stand it any longer, Mike pulled her into his arms. Cupping her face in his hands, he said, "I was a fool. Forgive me, I was such a blind fool."

Tears of relief streamed down her face as she felt the warmth of his arms back around her. His arms reached out to her, not out of pity or his sense of duty, but because he loved her.

Resting his forehead against hers, their breaths mingled as he spoke. She long to feel his lips on hers, but he still withheld them from her as he continued his apology.

"I was dying inside, wondering what you were feeling." Mike bent his knees a little so they were eye to eye, still cupping her face. His words were ragged as he tried to suppress his sobs. "I can't...I am terrified that when I touch you, I am hurting you. Am I stirring up the pain of your past every time I kiss you, touch you." Mike brushed her cheeks gently, tears rolling down his own cheeks. "Leanne, I would die to know that you were feeling that at my hands."

Leanne gripped the front of his shirt, and he felt a light shove as she sniffled. "You should have just asked me." Reaching between them, she brushed the tears from his cheeks.

"I know, I know." He whispered gently, turning his face to kiss her palm.

She threaded her fingers through the hair on the nape of his neck. "Mike, my past is dark and dirty, but you are, and have always been, everything that is beautiful and bright in my life. There has never been any fear with you, only hope."

"I am so sorry. I have dishonored you and our marriage wallowing in my own faulty thinking." His lips were hovering over her and he whispered. "Can you forgive me?"

"Yes." Leanne whispered, wondering why he wouldn't bridge the distance between their lips.

"You and God were having this wonderful walk toward redemption, and I missed out on that." He brushed his nose with hers.

Leanne could tell he was longing to kiss her, but he refused to make that move. He had hurt her, and he felt he didn't have to right to touch her. His next words confirmed it. "I am not worthy of your forgiveness."

"None of us are." With a moan of frustration, she closed the distance between their lips.

# Chapter Eighteen

"Rick!" Leanne shouted from the bathroom as the little boy came running through her room, tossing the ring pillow in the air. He was giggling as she picked him up. "You need to get your socks and shoes on, pronto." She sat him down on the bed and took the pillow from his hands. "Being a ring bearer is a big boy responsibility. So I need you to be ready for today. Go get your shoes and socks on, and then go wait for your dad in the living room."

Rick took off and Leanne walked down the hall to see how Karen was doing. She stopped just short of her doorway as she heard Mike softly speaking to her.

"...I understand it's loud and busy right now. We are all rushing around for Uncle Nate's wedding."

There was a stretch of silence before Karen spoke, her voice soft. "What if I fall?" Leanne could imagine that Karen was rubbing her earlobe.

"Remember, we counted the steps yesterday. I want you to just stay focused on each little step, count them down. And when you get to one, Grandma will take your hand and help you to your seat."

"Are you going to be at the end again, Daddy?"

"Yes I will, baby. Each step is one step closer to Mommy and Daddy."

There was another pause and then Leanne heard Karen's soft voice. "I can count down to get to you, Daddy."

"I know you can."

Leanne brushed a tear from her eye and headed back to the bathroom, not wanting to disrupt their talk.

Moments later, she saw him come up behind her. She smiled at him in the mirror, and he bent down and brushed a kiss against her bare neck. "You look beautiful."

Leanne turned around and straightened the bowtie on his tuxedo. "So do you."

He laughed. "Don't you mean handsome."

She shook her head. "No, I mean you look beautiful. Like a work of art, you are stunning and breathtaking."

Wrapping his hands around her waist, Mike pulled her closer to him and asked in a throaty growl. "What did I do to deserve such flattery?"

She didn't respond at first, then she leaned up on her toes and gave him a brief kiss. "You are an amazing father."

When she would have turned back to the mirror, he held her close in the circle of his arms. "You make me want to be an amazing father and an amazing husband."

She place a hand along his freshly shaven jawline. "How are you doing?"

He cocked his head to the side at the concern that tinged her voice.

"I saw the sadness in your face last night during the rehearsal every time you glanced at Pastor James."

"I wish it was my dad up there, I'm not going to

lie."

She cupped his face. "I know you miss him."

He bent his head to kiss her, but just shy of her lips, he pulled back at the sound of Karen's shrieks.

The little girl began screaming, "No, Rick!" repeatedly.

The two rushed to her room, and they found the toddler standing in the middle of Karen's room, tears pooling in his eyes and his lower lip retreating every time he sucked in a sob.

"What happened?" They both asked in unison.

"Don't get your dress dirty, baby." Karen said a couple of times in a row.

Mike and Leanne looked at each other. They knew she reverted to echolalia every time she was upset. Leanne bent down and examined the girl's dress. There weren't any stains or tears. "Your dress is fine."

After a few moments, the girl seemed to calm. "Rick was running."

Leanne felt Mike's hand on her shoulder as he spoke to Karen. "And we told you two not to run around and get your clothes dirty."

Mike picked up the little boy. "Why don't I take this little man to the church with me? That way you ladies can get ready in peace."

Standing, she kissed him, thanking him silently.

Two hours later, Leanne stood at the back of the church.

Mike turned and winked at her, before he escorted both the bride and the groom's mothers to their seats.

Kristina had chosen to have her bridesmaids walk up by themselves since she herself was walking alone. Leanne was behind Barbara, and as she made the short trip down the aisle, her eyes locked with Mike's.

When she completed her short trip up the aisle, she took her place next to Barbara, followed by Lisa, Kristina's matron of honor.

A collective "aw" rolled through the church as Rick and Karen came down the aisle. Tears stung the back of her eyes as she looked at her children. Rick came first, his little chest puffed out. When he got to the front, Mike gave him a thumbs up, which Rick tried to return, nearly toppling the ring pillow in the process.

When Leanne turned her attention back to Karen, she saw that her eyes were focused solely on Mike. With each step, she tossed a handful of ivory rose petals, and mouthed "One, two, three..." She turned to Mike, but the smile froze on her lips. Her darling husband was silently counting with his daughter, cheering her with each number he mouthed.

*Thank you, God.* Leanne prayed. *I know I am not worthy of all You have blessed me with, but I am thankful for Your love, Your mercy and Your grace.*

Laughter rumbled through the crowd as Karen took Sandra's hand and whispered none too softly. "I did it, Grandma!"

All laughter died as Kristina stepped out into the aisle way. She held a small white Bible along with her bouquet of white roses mixed in with greenery.

While they were planning the wedding, Kristina had said, "I don't have an earthly father to give me away, but my heavenly father has placed me in Nathan's life. The Bible will represent His presence with us during the wedding, but also in our marriage going forth."

Now, seeing her float down the aisle, and after all Leanne and Mike had been through, Leanne understood her choice.

Mike's eyes never left Leanne's throughout the rest of the ceremony. Leanne was sure he was silently repeating the vows as she was.

Later, at the reception, as Mike led her onto the dance floor, his words confirmed her suspicions.

"With all the craziness this morning, I don't think I got to tell you how beautiful you look." He brushed back a strand of hair that had fallen over her forehead. Mike cradled her face gently in his hand. "Do you remember our first dance?"

Leanne nodded, her voice tangled with so much emotion she couldn't speak.

"I brushed back this same strand of hair, and said I couldn't wait to do that for the rest of our life."

Her eyes misted over, but she flashed him a jaunty smile. "I'm still up for that if you are."

He kissed her gently on the forehead and then looked down intently in her eyes. "Later that night, you thanked me for loving you."

"You said you always would."

The words had barely left her mouth when he stated, "And I have. Even when I was confused and hurt, trying to surface from my jumbled emotions, I have always loved you."

"Me, too."

"My dad told me once that if we settle for only God's will in our lives, then we will be settled in our spirits, no matter what. I am making a new promise to you today. I won't settle for anything less than God's will in our lives, in our marriage, and for our family. And I promise to always be a reflection of His love."

Tears stung her eyes, and he brushed it back before if even fell on her cheek.

"I promise to not just wash you with words of love, but also with the truth and strength of His word. I promise to encourage, love and guide you with His word."

Leanne stretched up on her toes to brush a brief kiss on his lips, before she whispered, "I wouldn't settle for anything less."

## More from the author

**The LORD is close to the brokenhearted; He rescues those whose spirits are crushed. (Psalm 34:18 NLT)**

**Miracles in Disguise**
Book One

**Consider the Thorns**
Book Two

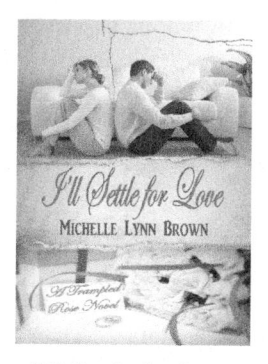

**I'll Settle for Love**
Book Three

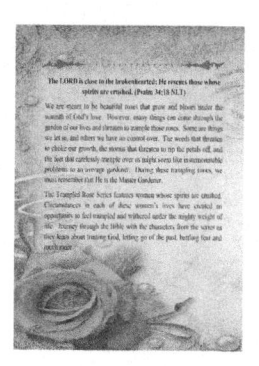

**The Trampled Rose Devotional**

(Coming Soon)

Want to discover new Christian authors?

Join the

**Christian Indie Author Readers Group**

on Facebook.

Opportunities for free books and giveaways.

https://www.facebook.com/groups/291215317668431/

Made in the USA
Coppell, TX
07 January 2021